Women of a Certain Age

WOMEN OF A CERTAIN AGE

Colleen Klein

To Dymphna Cusack

Elissa Campbell is a woman of a type which has become increasingly less fashionable in this liberated age. The use of wiles and artifice as a sexual ploy tends now to be regarded as disreputable. Nevertheless, women of Elissa's kind, women whose flirtatiousness masks a steely ambition, do still exist and exert their sway.

All characters and settings in this novel are imaginary. No persons, living or dead, are in any way depicted

First published in Great Britain in 1986 by
Century Hutchinson Ltd
Brookmount House, 62-65 Chandos Place,
London WC2N 4NW

Century Hutchinson Publishing Group (Australia) Pty Ltd
16-22 Church Street, Hawthorn, Melbourne, Victoria 3122

Century Hutchinson Group (NZ) Ltd
32-34 View Road, PO Box 40-086, Glenfield, Auckland 10

Century Hutchinson Group (SA) Pty Ltd
PO Box 337, Bergvlei 2012, South Africa

Reprinted 1987

ISBN 0 7126 9479 X

Printed and bound in Great Britain by
Anchor Brendon Limited, Tiptree, Essex.

1

AUSTRALIAN ACTRESS IN NUDE ROMP. JESS SCORES AGAIN. Black and foreboding, the headlines sprang out at Elissa Campbell. She sucked in her breath, put her fingers to her forehead and discovered there the corrugations of a frown. She arrested herself: frowning, scowling, both were taboo. She folded the newspaper in two and set it down on the table.

In a little while, she reflected, I might be able to pick it up again and read all about it, as they say; come to grips with all those degrading details of my daughter's public venture into prostitution. But first of all I've got to get hold of myself. She looked down at her hands, surprised to see them knotting and unknotting. Stupid, really, to be so distressed.

"I must keep cool," she said aloud. And she stepped in her light, swift fashion from the ordered blue-grey of drawing-room to the ordered grey-blue of kitchen, where the ritual of making coffee would surely calm her, or at least distance her from those quite disgusting headlines.

The kitchen, with its squat yellow dresser, housing the china used by four generations of Campbells, with its yellowish wall-clock that had ticked away their lives, with its thick scrubbed table, its windows discreetly admitting the winter sun — the kitchen awaited her, its mistress. Mistress of each heavy silver spoon, each heavy, dull-gleaming saucepan. How immeasurably petty it all seemed to her today. So this was the fate the gods had in store: keeper of the spoons. Not even spoons I chose myself, she thought mutinously, but mine by inheritance. It came to me pawed-over, all that dower, and like a greedy child I ran towards it, I couldn't wait to get my hands on it. Hard to believe. When Jim's mother died I rejoiced to think it was all mine. Brainwashed, I suppose, married out of the schoolroom, a mother before I finished my own growing up. Whatever Jim told me, I took as gospel. Queen, I thought I was queen. Elissa

Campbell of Rosencrantz. Queen of nowhere. I must have been mad.

Suddenly weak, Elissa sat down and lit a cigarette. No doubt about it, I've made a mess of things. The truth is, I don't think much of them, my daughters, one so fierce, one so watery. All nature's doing. I was so damn fertile, two babies in less than a year. One I'd have come to terms with — but before I could blink there was another one, that ginger-haired harridan up there on stage, stripping off her clothes for all comers to goggle at. Always like that. Elissa Campbell felt again the familiar surge of fury and frustration that Jess alone could provoke in her. Could and did, year in, year out. Jess at the garden party, falling into the lily pond, peeling off her soggy finery, pealing with wild laughter. Elissa tightened her lips at the memory of four year old Jess, scrawny and plain and arresting, bursting naked through the bank of cream cannas, ginger hair flattened on her narrow skull, hell-bent on stealing the show. Which she did. Jim, abashed and proud, scooping her up. Her green stare of triumph over his shoulder as he bore her off. Laughter and dire predictions. Jessica's first smash hit.

Elissa's face was hot, too hot. Oh God, all I need is the menopause to make my cup run over. I wish I had a son, she thought suddenly; compulsively. I can't stand the thought of what I've spent myself on: that vixen, prancing, and that slattern, holed up with her draggletail brood. In spate now, she found it impossible to stop. Like biting on a sore tooth. Leave it alone, she told herself; but no, she was bound to keep on, goaded by an irritation so intense that it approached hatred. I detest their manners and I deplore their looks. Put the three of us in a room, side by side, and I'd still outshine them, even now. But — for all that — they've reached their destinations, both of them. They saw which paths they were meant to take and they made a beeline. And here am I, not one step taken along my path. At forty three, more of my life behind me than there is to come. And I've done nothing, nothing. Reached nowhere.

The coffee, hissing, announced itself. The routine task of making it had brought her closer to tranquillity. She heard her breathing quieten, watched her smooth fingers move with their accustomed deftness as they lifted, poured, stirred. Thank God she had the whip hand over her body again. Today of all days she needed to be mistress of herself, to be ready with the airy gestures and deprecating laughter when her friends — her dear friends — summoned last week to luncheon today, opened their purses to bring out the cuttings from the papers which they had so considerately saved for her. Nonsensical, this whole birthday bit. Which one of them had started it, and when, and why? Long past time to be done with it.

She picked up her white cup and saucer, sniffing in the delicious, half-bitter tang. As with so many things, anticipation outshone fulfilment. Coffee. Lovemaking. Children. She looked out through the window to the garden, the freckles of pale sunshine on green leaves gently moving, the bees tipsily about their labours in the winter jasmine. All in all, the seasons rarely disappoint me, she thought. Just as I begin to feel bored with jonquils, the camellias make their bid. And by the time I'm tired of their lack of fragrance, the freesias have taken over. Somewhere I read — maybe someone told me — some Chinese saying — How did it go? Marry a girl and be happy a night, kill a pig and be happy a week, plant a garden and be happy forever. Only I'm not happy.

When I first heard that, oh I was happy then. I told Jim and he shook his head. They've got it all wrong, he told me. And he laughed and put down his thesis and took off his glasses and lifted me up. And tripped over Kass. Both of them howling, Jim's face all scratched, he'd die of blood poisoning, he'd murder that bloody cat. Shut up, you clot, I said under my breath; and I ran to get the antiseptic. As Casanova he made a good teaching fellow. Yet we were happy. And he improved with practice.

In the drawing-room the grandmother clock chimed, eleven times over. Hurry then. Swallow the coffee, stop brooding and get on with what has to be done before the influx.

The Campbells had never cared for doorbells. So it was the ancient, inefficient brass knocker that announced the first, too-early comer. All was in readiness, however: all things awaited. Lightfoot, she sped through the hall to open the door, to throw it wide-open and welcoming. It was Meg standing there. With a familiarity beyond cursory lip-to-cheek kisses, those ghost kisses of ladies on show, Elissa greeted Jim's sister, giving smile for smile. They stood a pace apart, the better to make their survey. Meg was perceptibly thinner, about a stone less than she'd been on her last visit, the remaining eight stone got up in pants of pale pink velvet and a magenta cashmere top. Meg worked very hard at her image: career woman, owner of a model agency, near-owner of the models she purveyed. She did not exert herself at her secondary role; the job of wife and mother limped in a poor second. The older and scruffier her children got, the younger and more exquisitely groomed their mother. Now, with her hair shaped in a golden helmet, with her new svelteness (although the big Campbell behind was still in evidence) she looked, at first glance, about twenty five; upon closer scrutiny, about thirty. She was, as Elissa knew, forty three and four months.

"Hi, Elissa, my love," she was carolling now, in the breezy, insouciant way she had adopted as part of her image. "I came early to help with the horse doovers and all that jazz."

Her slang was outdated. She had had the same problem as a girl, Elissa remembered. Somebody ought to tell her the facts, that outmoded catchwords date you as much as the Afro hairdo you left behind.

"It's all under control, Meg. I did it all yesterday, and tied the loose ends up this morning." Elissa moved the blackamoor a fraction, so that he would act as a doorstop. The outlandish agility of his pose never failed to amuse her. He stood forever on his hands, forever supporting on his feet a round crock, which she filled, at all seasons, with massed cream freesias, or, as now, with white jasmine. She patted the cascade of blossom into more careful disarray and stood back, pleased with the effect.

Meg looked on. "How absolutely fantastic to be able to pick masses of jasmine all the year round. You're so lucky to have this big garden. If only I'd been born a boy," Meg lamented.

"I think it's piffling," retorted Elissa, deliberately tart. She was sick of Meg's constant visits to the wailing wall. "Anyway you'd only have been the second son, you'd have missed out." She smiled, to take the sting out of her words: not a good idea to provoke Meg, with that erratic temper of hers. "Aren't you thin! Your waist's hardly there at all. Watch it though, don't lose any more or it'll start to come off your neck."

They measured glances, in which respect and dislike mingled. Long years before, after many skirmishes, they had decided against spending themselves, vainly, in total warfare.

"Hardly lost anything off my derrière," Meg mourned, getting in first. "Still, that's the way the cookie crumbles."

Another of her outworn phrases. Some day I'll risk it and tell her, Elissa vowed. But then, of course, she'll be unbearably up to date from then on. Better leave well alone. She looked at Meg, standing with feet planted, arms folded across her chest, propping up the door. "Come inside, Meg. You look like a charity collector hovering there." She walked ahead to the long drawing-room where, she thought suddenly, Meg had played the piano, had carried in the bowls of flowers, leaned through swags of wisteria to wave to her downy-faced beaux on the tennis court. No wonder she fumes, thought Elissa, and for no good reason she shivered.

"That couch will never wear out," stated Meg. "Three generations at least, heavens, it's barbaric. I like your new covers. Velvet, though. Will they wear?"

"As well as your pants. Better, probably." Elissa's voice was silky. "It's very heavy. Too heavy, really. What'll you have Meg?"

"Gin and ginger. No, make it tonic." She took her drink and sipped it, her bird-bright Campbell eyes, brown and unblinking, raking over the room. "Oh, is that a Brett Whiteley? Nice, isn't it? Cost the earth, I suppose."

"I don't know what it cost. Jim bought it for himself. It reminded him of something. Matisse, perhaps." Her voice was mocking. Jim, the dilettante collector.

Meg's eyes glinted, in a moment hard as flint. "You'll lose him if you're not careful. You're just too damn casual."

"No chance," drawled Elissa, deliberately insolent, inhaling slowly, puffing out, looking Meg over. No doubt her sister-in-law was distrait, unable to sit still, on her feet now and restlessly pacing. "What's wrong, Meggie?"

Meg shot her a glance, opened her mouth, then decided to close it. She began to walk aimlessly around the room, stopping to pat at her sleek hair before the long glass that had stood in its place for donkeys' years. There was something in the way she moved the jug of flowers, Lorraine Lee roses, marginally to the right then infinitesimally to the left, which asserted ownership. Elissa, in her turn, moved restlessly.

Then Meg swung round, her mouth pursed. Two whistle lines appeared above her top lip. "Why should anything be wrong?"

"No reason. But you seem shaken up. And for you to come early — or even to come at all — We count ourselves blessed if we even sight you these days."

"Oh well —" Meg tossed off her drink and set it down on the marquetry table. "Mother of pearl, pretty, isn't it. I always had a thing about that table."

"Meg. They'll all be here in a minute. So — what's wrong? That's if you did come to get something off your chest."

Meg's enamelled face crumpled. "The kids are being rotten. Angus dropped out of university. I just found out. But he hasn't been there since Easter." Her face was miserable, suddenly small

12

with misery.

"What's he doing now?" Elissa asked, after a silence.

"Bludging, what else. Mucking around with his guitar. And Sandy's sleeping with her boyfriend. I found the pill in her room when I went in looking for aspirin." She sat down.

Elissa was sorry. Under her spoiled, do-it-my-way-or-else antics Meg was a warm-hearted woman, or girl, fond of her husband and children. If she manipulated or bullied them, it was because they bowed the neck. Family and money had given her authority; good looks coupled with drive compounded her determination to rule at all costs. We are two of a kind, Elissa reflected, but she uses a bludgeon and I — what do I use? — a stiletto? Something Latin and sneaky, I suppose.

"I think they're both doing the in-thing, or whatever they call it now," Elissa ventured, after a long moment, punctuated only by the clock's heavy ticking. "Many boys do take a year off. And many schoolgirls are on the pill, I'm sure." Looking down at the bent head of Jim's young sister, she saw the fine streak of brownish-grey where the new hair was beginning to grow out. Meg seemed at once vulnerable, in need of reassurance and support.

She was crying now, mascara making dark streaks down her cheeks. "I'm terrified Angus is on drugs," she whimpered. Then she cleared her throat and blew her nose. "He's keeping rotten company. I don't know what to do."

"Can you have it out with him?" Elissa was at a loss for words of comfort. Troubles come in all shapes and sizes, she thought. "Look, it's probably just pot, if it's anything. Maybe you're just imagining it, anyway? No? Well, pot isn't addictive, is it?"

Meg gave another honk into the white linen square. Her voice was thick. "It's what it leads to that frightens me. The boys he knocks around with, they're all on the fringes of a ring. Pat's boy was in it. Did you know they found him dead up north?"

Elissa shook her head. Since Patty Best had left Banksia Ridge they had lost touch with her, the only one of the little girls, playmates first, then schoolfriends, who had gone away and stayed away. For the others, they came and went, abroad sometimes, on skiing vacations often, selling up sometimes and moving slightly outwards to the perimeter. But always coming back.

"Pretty awful," said Elissa, remembering Pat, so proud of the little boy in the stroller, Rufus, she called him. Even as a baby, a wild little boy. She moved impatiently, anxious to be done with these sour tales, refusing to let herself be harrowed. "What can I do, Meg? Would you like Jim to talk to Angus?"

"No, he wouldn't listen. He's anti-establishment. He says he is, anyway. But if ever you get a chance, will you do what you can? He doesn't think you're a fuddy-duddy. And he knows you like him."

"Oh I do. I've always adored him. He was the most angelic baby, like a little brown gumnut. I hated being the mother of girls. Plain girls. Well, one plain and one fat." The words hung in the air between them.

Meg sat straighter, shooting a queer sideways glance at Elissa before she spoke. "Really? I always suspected it. You should have kept on going."

"Too late now." Elissa was surprised to detect wistfulness in her voice. "I'd probably have ended up with half a dozen of the same."

"— So will you, Liss? Talk to Angus, I mean. He's got a thing about what he calls women of a certain age." She caught Elissa's eye and they burst out laughing. "Oh, it's good to laugh," said Meg. "What a handle to give us." Her face grew doleful again, her fleshy lips drooping, sending the lines downward, adding years to her age. "I keep thinking it's all my fault. If I'd stayed home it wouldn't have happened. I'd have had my finger on the pulse."

"Like my non-existent son — It's too late now to talk about might-have-beens. Really, Meg, the best thing that could happen would be for him to shack up with some nice girl who'd get him

14

back on course."

"Where is she?" asked Meg. "If you run into her let me know, will you? I'd welcome anyone who'd get him off the grass and back between the rails. Joke." She swilled her second drink round the glass before she downed it. "Maybe this liberation bit's got its drawbacks."

"What hasn't?" Elissa's voice was dry. "You're more concerned about him than Alex."

"Well, yes. Sandy's pretty clued-up. Girls are, I think. Look at Jess!" she cried, the pink of happiness flooding her cheeks as she remembered that other people have their troubles too.

"Jess was abominable. It was a relief when she quit the house and gave NIDA the benefit of her tantrums. I was glad to be rid of her. And you know Jean was nearly as bad. Even more idiotic, really." Elissa bit her lip, recalling the absurdity of that time, Jeanie lumbering around at the beck and call of a wild boy, still wet behind the ears. The memory of that wedding, with the bride so advanced in pregnancy, the groom so reluctant, could still make her quiver with distaste. "That revolting wedding, I wish I could forget it. Jean cajoled her father behind my back, little wretch —" Children, how they disappoint you. And yet without them the house seems too big for us. "You know, Meg, the house seems very empty. Even if the kids still worry you, they're still there. There's a reason for keeping the house going," she said reflectively. "Sometimes I wonder about the empty years ahead," she added, because, after all, one good confession deserves another.

"You'll manage." Meg was more cheerful now that she'd feasted on somebody else's troubles. "And at least your kids aren't destroying themselves in front of your eyes. Making you feel guilty and miserable." She looked happy, not miserable at all, flashing the grin that made her mouth look like the slot of a letter-box. How like Jim she is, the square Campbell jaw, those square, long-lasting Campbell teeth. "What about Jess's latest prank? I bet Jim's got something to say."

"Oh, stiff upper lip, as usual. He was stunned when he opened the paper. But by the time he took off he was cracking hardy. He said he was proud of her blazing integrity."

"Christ he's mad!" cried Jim's sister.

"Is he ever!" cried Jim's wife. "But there'd be no stopping her, she's utterly set on her own way, she always was. Bull at a gate."

"Like you. There's not much of Jim in Jess. Jim's mulish." Meg took out her mirror, to assess damages and begin repairs. "She's just like you."

"Like me?" Elissa considered the words, glancing down at her hands, entwined on the amber challis of her dress. Big hands, unexpectedly big, considering her slenderness. Then she nodded. "Perhaps. Though God knows I've led the most innocuous of lives."

"Are you angry with her?" Meg persisted, leaning forward, not bothering to conceal her delight. "Everyone'll be gloating. I bet the lines have been running hot today." She gave a guffaw, another hand-me-down from the family coffers. "Do you know anything about the show?"

Elissa Campbell tried to speak dispassionately. "Not much. She kept it all to herself. I'm ashamed, in one way — Lesbian romp, for God's sake! Jess is the daughter, as far as I can make out. I think Sappho's got a bisexual lover as well as a coterie of girls. Or perhaps he's Jess's lover. But who does what with whom the papers didn't say."

Meg was lying back, helpless with laughter. The rich stuff of the chair, the gaudiness of her plumage, the gold cap of her hair all contrived to make her look bizarre: a cross between a macaw and a bon-bon.

She's carrying it a bit too far, Elissa judged. Relief at a friend's misfortune, that's one thing; but outright gaiety, that's another. What unspeakable luck, really, that my birthday coincided with the news. She spoke with some severity. "Of course, Meg, I don't approve, I don't have to tell you that. But I've got to hand it to her for throwing herself heart and soul into what she believes in.

And wants."

Meg was all at once bitter. "Kids," she said. "I wonder why we want 'em."

Mine were wished on me, thought Elissa, still, after all these years, vexed. "I didn't know any better," she quipped. "If I'd been a bit older I'd have made a better job of them. Perhaps." Perhaps you should be nudging thirty and done with your own growing up. Yes, that might have been better.

The garden outside was all at once chirping, a giant bird-cage. Meg sped to join the newcomers, for some reason of her own. Through the front courtyard they came stepping, half a dozen women, each one done up to outdazzle the rest. Bird-greetings were ousted by bird-chatterings, voices sweet or harsh that ran down the scale and up again. Laughter shivered and splintered. In pants woven in England, in tops from Afghanistan, in jersey suits from Italy they came, decked-out, towards Elissa, to mark her birthday (honour it, if you like) as she marked theirs. All those girls of the Christmas before last, the brides of two weeks ago, the young mothers of the day before yesterday. Where had the years gone? In an eyeblink, it seemed, they were middle-aged matrons. As I am, thought Elissa, in a panic, the palms of her hands all at once clammy.

Smiling, outwardly serene, she moved to greet them. Casually charming. "Hi, girls, what's new?" Clasping and being clasped, breathing in a miasma of assorted French perfumes, exclaiming over hair cut, hair curled, hair dyed to a rich chestnut or coaxed to a premature silver. Elissa Campbell, attending to all these debts, isolated by some new force of vision, shepherded her friends into the house.

"Happy birthday," they were chorusing, as they always did. "You look a year younger." That was the password. No presents, by request. Only reassurance.

With Meg's help, Elissa presented them with gin and sherry and brandy, in various guises and strengths; proffered nuts and olives and caviare and thin cheese straws. Then she sat down, swinging her legs to the correct angle, side by side, and surveyed them, those women of — how did Angus put it? — those women of a certain age.

Some had worn better than others, she observed; notably Meg and Annie. A couple had hit the bottle; Rhonda certainly, Helen perhaps. Two had survived hysterectomies. They all wore subdued lipstick, too pale for their teeth, no longer white, but, at best, ivory. Almost every one wore eyeshadow; some had added mascara. For that matter, so had she. Elissa blinked: we're mad, she thought, to attempt the courting display of the young. No excuse for it, really. No middle-aged rake in orbit, to be lured in and trapped. Unless — she fixed Rhonda with a thoughtful eye. Tom was said to be ready to take off. Could be that she was already working on a replacement. There was something out of kilter about Rhonda today. But then again, there always was.

Annie was brewing up a storm. She'd only dropped in for a weeny moment, to say happy birthday darl. Tall as a giraffe she stood, drinking her martini. No no, she couldn't be asked to sit, she was on the wing, sweetie. Ted had been posted overnight to America, she had to tear home and pack. She stood there long enough to show off her new Valentino, kissed Elissa, and was gone.

"I'll see myself out, sweet. I'll send you all postcards, or something. Bye now."

Annie had gone, but there were plenty left. The gap closed at once. Hostess, inescapably committed to charming and being charmed, Elissa composed herself, to listen. Inevitably, someone had just come back from abroad, voicing bitter complaints of tourists, crowds and foreign insolence. As well as Australian parochialism. Last year, she reminded herself, it was my turn to journey and hold court and boast. An inverted kind of boasting in which she refused to speak of the gardens that pleased her most; so that Bodnant remained unnamed, and Tresco Abbey; and the Generalife, that charmed word, never passed her lips. But Sissinghurst and Hidcote and lesser delights she was ready to share with the listening circle. Last year I was the one who skimmed like a dragon-fly over Europe's bounty of summer gardens, and came back dazzled and replete, with a head brimming with pictures and a heart crammed to bursting-point with envy.

This time it was — who was it? — it was Frances, just off the — what was it? — Trans-Siberian railway. In a pale cashmere suit, bought in Paris, Frances dragged at her cigarette and blew out hot air. "Raw life," she was breathing. "Oh, it was beyond all description. Russia! Stupendous! Next year, girls, put Moscow on your list. And Istanbul! Oh, those Turks!"

Everyone squealed at the mention of all those Turks. Frances rolled her pallid eyes while she hinted at unmentionable delights; her ugly face, with the skin dried out from too much golf and tennis, was quite aglow. So it seems she had a one night stand with some ancient carpet-dealer, Elissa surmised, sourly, or perhaps she bought herself a pretty, dissolute boy. She added her exclamations to the chorus.

Even as they oohed and ahed, Frances's listeners shifted infinitesimally; but good manners, as well as the rules, decreed that the traveller, returning, should be heard till her rhapsodies ran dry. Besides, next year someone else, some one of them, would be glad of the captive audience. So except for reminiscent laughs and sighs they let her run her course, unchecked. Out of the corner of her eye Elissa timed her on grandmother Campbell's grandmother clock: six minutes. Still, everything comes to an end, even travellers' tales. Not before time it was open slather for everyone who'd ever set foot in another country: for everyone present.

Rhonda commiserated with Frances for missing that exquisite little church at Parma. "Oh the frescoes," she sighed. "And Versailles — you didn't miss the tapestries, did you? I was stunned, literally stunned. Didn't you manage to squeeze in Versailles, Fran?"

"I was doing the East," Frances countered indignantly. "I told

19

you, I wanted to get away from the tourists in Europe."

They all joined in complaints about the masses of tourists jamming the Louvre. As for the Sistine Chapel, it had become too vulgar for words.

"Genoa is charming," Rhonda persisted. "Did you find time for Genoa?"

"I was doing the *East*," wailed Frances.

Elissa, refilling the glasses, heard them without any sense of involvement, as if she were light years away, as if Rhonda, Genoa's partisan, were a visitor from outer space.

"Don't you agree, girls, that Genoa is absolutely sui generis," she was insisting, showing off, her grey eyes cold, her pointy nose pointier than usual, determined to make it clear that she alone was capable of appreciating the uniqueness of — well, of whatever she happened to be on about. No wonder she's got through three husbands. No wonder those children, plumped down in boarding-schools, choose to go elsewhere for their holidays. Really, she's insufferable, thought Elissa, she always was. I wonder why we put up with her.

Rescue was at hand. At the door stood Bertha Mackintosh, bluff and hale and older by half a generation. "Sewer, you mean," she boomed. She beamed on all of them, this latecomer from one or another of her good works, dressed with the regal dowdiness that nobody dared to question. Her bachelor son continued to pay court to all of them. She's worn better than he has, reflected Elissa, accepting a forthright kiss on the cheek, a no-nonsense slap on the behind.

Bertha gripped a whisky and soda: her drink. "Italy's one vast sewer," she stated, her robust voice as full-bodied as her shape, her feet as firmly planted as a stone age goddess. "Hello, Helen, how's Charlotte?" Even at a luncheon party Bertha was on the job of facing life's unpleasant facts.

Helen Wilson, plump-faced, sweet and deeply sad, shook her head. "They're trying a new treatment," she said, her lips turning up in hope. "They think they might be able to shock her back into life. Since the baby died she just hasn't wanted to go on living."

Everyone was silent. Watchful of one another, as they always were, jealous and bitchy as they could be on occasion, they were united in pity for Helen's girl, Charlotte, who'd really copped it. First an illegitimate baby, then the baby dead, and now over the brink into madness.

"Keep your chin up Helen," advised Bertha, swallowing her drink at one go. "Shock treatment, eh? Hope they know what they're doing. A few volts too many and she's done for."

Deployed around chairs and sofas, the ladies listened to her with respect. Somehow nobody dared to give Bertha cheek. At their conclaves she was elder statesman. Stateswoman, as she'd put it.

Helen, however, fronted up. "No, it's something new. A sort of combination of drugs and group therapy. It's a matter of getting her back into the swing of life," she murmured, gently and humbly. "Little by little she should improve."

"I told you not to marry again," Bertha trumpeted, wiping her mouth with the back of her hand and fixing Helen with her shrewd, affable gaze. "I warned you, didn't I? I said you ought to wait till she got past puberty. Touchy time. Some girls take it in their stride. Some don't. You could see Charlotte'd make heavy weather of it. Still, while there's life there's hope." She held out her glass, tight-clasped in hands as strong and big as a wharfie's. Her beautiful tweed suit, tailored in London, had taken on her bulky shape. "Another of these, please, Elissa, m' dear. How does it feel to be forty three, eh? You're getting on. Not that you've packed up yet, not by a long shot. I've been feeding retarded babies all morning, poor little blighters. I'm utterly pooped."

The lines of fatigue and endurance on her face, deep-bitten, gave her the look of a totem. Detesting incapacity, deploring the unfit allowed to live on, she nevertheless went into every arena to help. Big Bertha, bossyboots, they called her behind her back. She had been a woman when they were all girls; she ruled them as she ruled her committees, by the simple assumption that she was born to rule. Cheque book at the ready, she was always on the spot, coping with the jobs that other women, less sturdy or more squeamish, hung back from. I really do take off my hat to her, thought Elissa, handing over the replenished glass: that toughness and ability to look any nastiness in the eye, how admirable. Yet — oddly — where her own son is concerned, she is blind and helpless.

Elissa stood smiling around her, breathing in a familiar mixture of roses and cigarette smoke and titivated ladies; listening to the ripple of their talk. Meg lit a cigarillo.

"Taken to cigars, have you, Meg?" quizzed Bertha. "Try one the proper size, not one of those weevils. Speaking personally, I like to finish my dinner with a good cigar."

The room shook with mirth, at Bertha's frankness, at Meg's discomfiture. They were all a bit jealous of Meg.

Now Bertha turned her attention back to Helen. "Well it's too late to change things now, Helen, you've made your mistake, let's hope it can still be remedied. That's why I never remarried after Duncan died, I thought I'd get the boy raised first." Her eyes grew soft and moist at the mention of her son. "I had my chances, you know, after my money, most of them, still you can make a worse kind of bargain. At least that way you know where you are. Just hold on to the purse-strings, that's all you've got to do, unloose them a bit at a time. Don't sign anything over and you'll stay in the box-seat. Well, I made the right choice. And by the time I got him reared I thought I was better off the way I was." She finished her whisky and smacked her lips. "Tell you the truth, I never got asked later on."

"Oh I did, just the other day." Kay extricated the stone from her mouth and held it in her finger-tips. She wasn't wearing nail-polish, the only one who wasn't. "Lovely olives, Elissa. — That young Italian gardener who was helping me with some pruning. Perhaps he didn't mean marriage, though. It was just a polite way of saying it, I'd like to marry you this minute, missus." She was chuckling to herself at the memory. Her skin had lined, but her eyes and her teeth were as good as ever. Now, with Philip dead and her four girls flown the coop (one married, two shacked-up, one abroad) she lived on alone in her decrepit, pretty little house and tended her garden. Expecting nothing much of life, she was rarely disappointed. "It's the first time I was propositioned since — oh I can't remember — yes I can. I had to go into town in a hurry to see about that lump in my breast. Before they sliced it off."

"Poor you," sighed Meg, her white hands with the magenta nails flying to her own breasts. "You must feel mutilated."

"I'm glad to be alive. After all, I've reared my babies. And there's no man to whinge."

"I'd die, I'd really die, Kay," said Frances. "I'd rather be dead than mutilated."

Kay turned on Frances a face that was suddenly stony. "I don't give a damn. Anyway you've had a hysterectomy. I guess you're mutilated too."

"Oh, they left the important bit alone," retorted Frances. "If you know what I mean."

Everyone laughed; everyone knew.

"There's a painting by Magritte," Elissa recalled. "It's a woman's face, but it's got two nipples for eyes, a navel for a nose and a triangle of pubic hair for a mouth. A man's eye view of women."

"Ain't it the truth!" yelled Rhonda.

Kay was sick of her story. Begged to go on, she gave a shrug. "Oh, it's nothing, really. My car broke down. An old lecher gave me a lift. Dirty old bugger. I couldn't shut him up. When he finally opened the door and let me get out, he gave me a juicy pinch on the bum."

United now, members of the women's club, they shared glee: what men wanted, they had. Sopranos and one contralto, they sent their laughter shivering up to the chandelier, to the long mural on the pale walls. Each one vied to be next to tell of her

23

magnetic power over men. In Italy, Meg had been pinched black and blue; in fact had been forced to call a doctor who in turn pinched her till she was purple. Blondes, of course, they bring out the beast in Latins.

"Oh, were you blonde then?" enquired Rhonda, all innocence. "I thought you were still brunette." She smoothed her auburn hair. "Those dagoes, I think they're worse with redheads. I was actually bleeding."

Voices jostled, rising and falling, as Rhonda, Frances, Meg, giving no quarter, took turns in embroidering, skiting, or just plain lying. Anything to get the limelight. Like Jess. Remembering her daughter, Elissa grimaced. No one had said a word on the subject. Yet.

All my friends, she mused, looking them over, listening to them, touching the stuff of their dress as she bent over them, replenishing their grog. We've all come to the end of our tether, or just about. We're all redundant. We've finished our jobs. Whether we like it or not, we're on the outskirts of life. Except Bertha — and Theo, she's still in the thick of it.

"Where's Theo?" she asked, suddenly bereft, looking around for the un-chic, un-svelte Theo, the eternal odd man out.

"She's gone to some athletic carnival to see the boys run or hurdle or break their legs, or something. She never stops running after those kids. As soon as swimming finishes then football starts or God knows what." Meg's tone was vicious. What's her stake in it, Elissa wondered, and was answered as Meg went on. "If she thinks she'll stem the tide by playing guardian angel, she's got another think coming. They'll turn out just as rotten as all the other kids in this generation. You'll see."

"She's riding for a fall." Frances chimed in. "She gives up everything for those two, how old are they now, thirteen or fourteen I suppose. She told me she keeps on that huge place because they like it. She could get a unit and really get something out of life. Thank God I never had any kids, that's what I always say when I see the mums wringing their hands."

24

She shot a glance at Helen then looked embarrassed. "Sorry, Helen, I didn't mean you. But for the life of me I can't see why she doesn't just pack them off to boarding-school and get herself a job."

"She's got a job, remember? Teaching swimming in that bloody great idiotic pool of hers."

"I think she just likes to have them home," ventured Kay. "I don't blame her. One day they're swinging in the gum trees and the next they're gone."

"She ought to think about getting married again before it's too late. So should you, Kay." Rhonda, just a bit drunk, was on the job again, giving free advice.

"No!" exclaimed Helen, violently.

They all fell silent, averting their eyes from her drawn face.

"Men, who needs them? They're utterly dispensable," stated Bertha. "Except for breeding."

"What about Sam?" asked Elissa, slyly.

Bertha came back fast. "Oh, I except sons." She took off for the lavatory.

"We all except sons. That's why they grow up to be husbands." Rhonda sounded bitter, as she always was when one of her marriages was folding up. Everyone knew that Tom was a rag on every bush. No one, however, mentioned it, since no one wished to be torn limb from limb. Soon, no doubt, Tom would be given his marching orders, like the two who went before him.

Elissa found herself more restive by the minute. How footling, all these gatherings that had been going on for years. So dreary. So God-damn repetitive. Buttering up. Backscratching. Backbiting. I don't think I can stand another hour of it. And I've got thirty years lined up, with the grave yawning at the other end. There must be some way out, there's got to be something worth trying at. Worth believing in.

She moved restlessly. "Sometimes I think I've missed out on something basic." Her gaze ranged over the rugs from Persia, the sombre richness of curtains, the sheen of polished wood. I'm in prison, she thought. I want to get out and I don't know how. I don't like my life any more.

"Shame on you," scolded Kay. "Your lovely girls. And those adorable grandchildren."

"Jess made quite a splash. Aren't you excited about it?" Rhonda was purring, her little cat's face alight with malice, her slitted grey eyes probing. She selected a cashew nut, and stared at it before she popped it in her mouth, to be demolished by her newly-capped teeth.

In the hush stirred only by their breathing, the winter roses gave up their pale scent. And they all waited, all her good friends. Her birthday was the reason for their coming; but this scandalous morsel was their reward.

"Excited?" Elissa lifted her eyebrows. "Oh, hardly. I think she's admirable and degenerate, both. In equal amounts." Her voice was low and very precise, a trick she had learned from Jim when he wanted to press home a point. "I think it must be very heady to want something so much that you'll do absolutely anything to get it. But I deplore that kind of public stripping."

"I thought you'd be mortified," suggested Rhonda, still hopeful.

Kay was enthroned as first comforter, as always. "She always was a little tigress. Like you, Elissa."

"Like me? By comparison I'm a Siamese cat." Elissa swooped down to the ottoman and caught Ka up in her arms. She looked over his little dark head at her circle of friends (who needs enemies?) and she nodded at them. Her head felt very light and clear. They were determined to commiserate and she was determined to outwit them. "I can't help admiring her fury. It's ages since I felt impelled to do anything at all. I wonder — are we all redundant when we stop having any real goal?"

"Speak for yourself!" cried someone.

"Come off it, Lissa!"

"Oh Elissa, don't be so mean!"

Elissa cut through the din. Give them something to think

about, get them hot under the collar, then they'd forget about Jess. Who was, after all, her daughter, not their prey. "We're so unimportant. Our schemes are so piffling, don't you think? It wouldn't matter if someone said poof and we all disintegrated, would it? We've brought up our children. Our husbands could replace us in six months — oh, alright, a year, then. There's nobody depending on us. We don't matter."

Bertha was back, her petticoat hanging on one side, coffee-coloured Alençon lace showing. She bridged the silence. "Oh, if it comes to that, nothing in the world matters," she pronounced. "But I'm not ready to turn it in yet, Elissa Campbell. And I want my fodder. I can't stay long. I've got to get back to my sewing. Fifty dog coats to cut out for the Blind Babies' Appeal. Yes, I said fifty, no more or less. And I need refuelling."

"We all do!" they called, as the clock struck one.

"I smell garlic bread," said Frances.

Food, they all wanted food. When they weren't gorging, they were on diets. I've got to get off this treadmill somehow, vowed Elissa, in despair.

But first things first. The soufflé would be all but ready, the borsch needed only sour cream. "In you go," she bade them lightly.

They rose then from their couches, leaving the imprint of their bodies on the cushions. Silken and scented, curled and creamed, past first youth (and second youth too, for that matter) but still fighting the good fight against age, they stepped or strolled or pranced towards the dining-room, making for the food that would stoke them, the wine that would set their tongues to ever more furious wagging.

Well it came to an end, in the end. And they all went home.

She stacked the dishwasher. Tomorrow Mrs Tate would come, in overall and bandanna, and remove all traces of the bidden guests. The strange sensation that had possessed her was with her still; a compound of frustration and boredom and nausea. Probably just a mood, she told herself. The luncheon party seemed a summary of her whole life; cushioned and repetitious. Deep in her bones she knew that it was more than a mood, that it sprang from some desperation, deep-seated, and that something would have to be done about it.

She stepped into the dooryard beyond the kitchen, into a place striped with winter's timid afternoon sunshine. Sambac jasmine, sweet and acrid. Cumquats in tubs: pretty enough. Before her eyes stretched the green haunts of lawn and bullbay trees, before her feet the long walk to the sandy cove, beneath the knotted branches of the wisteria. She liked the wisteria walk, one of the few effects on a grand scale. She had extended and embellished it, so that now it divided to encircle a folly and culminated in what might be called a vista of bay. What I could have done with a big whack of land, she mused. One and a bit lousy acres, it gives you no scope at all.

Today I'm going to feel whatever I want, to hell with censoring everything I say and think. It's just too petty for words, anyone with an eye for space or grandeur — anyone less concerned with money than those stingy Campbell men and their bleating wives would have hung on to half — or a tenth — or even a fiftieth of what they started with. If I had — oh, even ten acres — I could do something really spectacular with this garden. As it is I'm hamstrung. Of course the Generalife isn't big, but the terrain bellies it out. You can do so much more with a hilltop garden. God I'm a malcontent, she chided herself. Listen to me. Flat gardens are no good. Sons are better than daughters. I'm jealous of Jessica, I'm jealous of anyone with something to live for.

Shaken, she shuttled from one green enclave to another, some that she had refurbished, some that she had been instructed to leave alone, some that she had been, amazingly, allowed to initiate. I was a fool, she thought, I had all the power in the world then. I could have made Jim do anything I wanted, handed the house over to Meg, started again somewhere else. But I loved the house then, I'd have died before I left it. It's only lately that it's all gone sour.

Something thudded against her ankle: Ka. She bent to pick him up, her heart swelling with love for him. Yet loving him, she had rendered him neuter. To save him from those wounds he limped home with, that kept him forever at the vet's. But perhaps I did it so that I could reign alone — oh, that's stupid, reign over a cat. My dynasty: grandmother and mother and son. And I love him most of all. The girls begged for a dog. No, I said, a dog killed his mother. Never. After a while they stopped asking. Another mistake, I suppose. Today I hardly know myself, I've got myself muddled or lost, what Rhonda calls all ballsed up.

Who am I, really? Perhaps Kay's right. Perhaps I really am like that stringy girl up on stage with her skinny legs and her quiff of — I suppose — ginger hair. Unless she's shaved it off, if that's the cult. Whatever's required, she'll do it, she'll stop at nothing. Nor would I, if I were young in this generation. No way I'd be chatelaine of a homestead, mistress of a gentleman turned professor to fill in the blank of his days.

Oh God I'm bitter, she berated herself. I'm bored and I'm bitter and I'm the dregs. But I'll have to find a way out or I'll cave in.

2

Cocooned against all impacts from the world outside the four white walls, Elissa Campbell lay between sleep and waking. Dawn prised at the frail silk of the curtains. Another day. I might just lie here all day long, swaddled like a mummy, she thought, still muzzy with sleep, opening her eyes, then shutting them. The clove scent of the stocks outside the window prickled her nose. She sneezed twice.

The long lump in the bed pulled over against hers, the lump shaped like a dead body, did not stir. In sudden panic — for men have been known to die in their sleep — she reached out and touched him, bending over his carved face. No, alive. He groaned and dug his head deeper into the pillow.

"Sleep on," she muttered, wide awake now, clasping her hands behind her head, staring up at the dusky convolutions of the ceiling, which would reveal itself, at first light, as garlanded with plaster roses and cherubim. Whose whimsy was that, she wondered. Today's woman, indulging her caprice, would have a mirror there to reflect her high jinks. The Victorian (Edwardian?) lady plumped for cabbage roses and babies with round rumps. She would ask Jim, he'd know which one of the Campbell bleaters summoned an artist, or artisan, to festoon her ceiling with roses. And Elissa, she in turn had left her imprint: a bedroom all white, great white bed (two beds masquerading as one) white silk cushions, white wallpaper faintly shot with silver. Very vestal virgin. Daylight, when it came, would reveal the ceiling as palest pink. She had thought the room exquisite; she had run her hands voluptuously over the subtly differing textures, been charmed by the varying shades of white. Now she thought it pretentious. Jim, however, liked it very much. Perhaps it was his ambition to deflower a virgin afresh each night, she surmised, and smiled to herself. For in this one area they had never reached satiety. She had contrived to preserve a degree of aloofness, which continued to intrigue him. Her ready participation held almost always an element of detachment. But sometimes it changed and bouts of ardent coupling surprised them both, or rough and tumble bouts amused them both.

Elissa, sometimes toying with the thought, found no taste in herself for adultery. As for Jim, whatever detours or indiscretions there had been, he kept them to himself. She knew that the girls he lectured to were often on the prowl. He was only human. Once, she was sure, he had succumbed; twice, perhaps. The extra care with which he dressed, the sneaky gleam behind his glasses, the shifting, guarded quality of his conversation gave him away. Still, twenty five years is quite a span. And he came back from his sorties so contrite and so amorous, so relieved that it had all been kept under wraps, so certain that she was oblivious, that she was content to let him dream on. The next sabbatical after his lapse turned out to be a second honeymoon. Her lips turned up, pleased to be remembering; all those pleasant daytime encounters in this dark room, with the blinds drawn and the girls playing outside in their treehouse, were only a prelude. Pubs in Cornwall; a castle in Scotland, under a fat red eiderdown; palazzos in Venice. I could write a book on them, all the ways and means the clever young think that they've invented: nothing new under the sun, really. How strange, never one slip-up. If the cap fits, wear it, I said to Jim once, twirling it round on my finger-tip — how old were we then? I was thirty-one, he was thirty-five. Throw the bloody thing away, he said. And I said no. We palmed the girls off on Aunt Winifred. And we never gave them a thought.

Forty-seven, now, almost. Yes, he's looking older, thought Elissa, watching his face as the daylight sharpened. Lines fanned out from his eyes, the flesh clung less tightly to the bone. All in all though, he's held up well. The crisp reddish hair was as thick and curly as ever; grizzled, of course, but it suited him. Without the glasses that detracted from his looks, lying there, eyes closed, he looked impressive, very. Many women would envy me. A man so well set up in every way and so (on the whole) inescapably mine. Enough money. Enough looks, both of us. We're all dressed up and no place to go. So what am I to do? Twiddle my thumbs and settle in, as Kay suggested, to being a grandmother? Bored already with the day not even begun, she leaned over and faute de mieux, blew gently in his big whorled ear.

He reacted; snorting, tossing his head, then reaching for her. His lips, practised, framed a gallantry. "Milly," he whispered. Short for Millamant, his bookish bed-name. His more instinctive self thrust towards her in confident expectation. His hands, reaching out, managed to snaffle one of her breasts. "Fielded," he said, indistinctly, and he rubbed the stubble of his chin against the smoothness of her face.

It was all very déjà: the mixture as before. Bang on her period, she'd take a chance. Thrust and parry, come into my parlour, my syrupy parlour.

"What did you say?" he asked, already halfway there.

"I said come into my syrupy parlour."

"Thank you." He smiled down at her. "Don't mind if I do."

Elissa lay, languidly basking, allowing him to make the pace. From long and dedicated practice each knew the other's needs. They had long ago worked out the hows and whats and whens.

"Aly Khan," she teased him. "You're as practised as Aly Khan." And had no more to say until his weight began to bother her. Then she gave him a push to say get going; a hitch of the hips first, then an impatient movement of shoulder. In a minute he would bestow on her the ritual kiss. She was reminded of a vaudeville joke, very crude.

"What's the difference between a pianist and a penis?" she asked him.

"Tell me."

"Well, it's screamingly funny. One tickles the ivories and the other tickles the ovaries. I don't know which, though."

He gave her a grin, then a light kiss. He resumed his place in the bed next to hers, first towelling himself with his pyjama top, as he always did, then dropping it on the floor. Déjà, everything déjà. "Better be getting up," he told her, not budging.

"James." Again she linked her hands behind her head, grateful to him because for a while he'd stopped her from thinking. "James, do you realize that we've been doing what we were doing for twenty five years. A quarter of a century. Do you realize that makes —" she calculated — "nearly three thousand times. More, if you count nearly every minute when we first got married."

"So?" He pulled on his pyjama pants and swung out of bed. "Is that good or bad?"

"Well, good, I suppose. You've improved. Jim, remember those upside-downers and inside-outers and stander-uppers? Lord they were uncomfortable, weren't they? No wonder you've got so adept. When I was looking at that sex book that awful Nora left at Jeanie's, I kept thinking we'd tried everything." She was chattering now, anxious to keep him with her.

He dallied, scratching his bare back. "What was Nora doing with a book like that ? She's not married, is she?"

"Oh, that doesn't mean a thing. You must know that. All the girls like to develop their expertise now. Especially ones like that Nora. So unkempt and ugly. No wonder she's always being dumped."

"I thought she was rather touching," he said. "The little I saw of her. Lovely figure. She's got a good mind too." He began his deep breathing exercises, over by the window.

"A born loser." Elissa refused to praise another woman, even a hobgoblin like Jeanie's pal. "Jim," she asked suddenly. "What do you feel about Jess? I mean really and truly, not just putting on a front." He hadn't mentioned her last night, not a word, all the way through the birthday dinner and birthday theatre. "Quick, before you start reasoning."

He frowned. Standing arrested in the first thin shaft of sunlight he looked knobbly-kneed and unsure of himself, like

33

the young man she had married.

"I'm not sure," he answered slowly. "Well, I was staggered, of course. It's not easy to take, the thought of your daughter up there in front of the groundlings."

"All with hard-ons."

He moved sharply, discomforted. She had touched the tender spot.

"Don't be coarse. Actually, I don't think it's prurient. It's a kind of send-up of sex."

"Want to bet?" asked Elissa, scornfully.

"I suppose whether we like it or not, it's the manner of the times."

"The only thing, she's pretty scrawny. They might think she's a boy."

He pretended not to hear. He started on the next set of exercises, squatting. "Go and get me some breakfast, like a good girl."

"In a minute. When I've had a shower." Slippery in the thighs, that familiar feeling. Pleasant, unpleasant, which? Both, probably. Prostitutes, they'd be eternally awash. She lifted up her mass of hair, then let it fall back on her neck. Good hair, thick, not grey at all. One of these days, though, she'd get it cut. "I really couldn't be bothered with lovers," she said aloud, watching him touch his toes.

He stopped then. He looked across at her, biting back a grin, as was his habit. It was a habit that had sent his mouth slightly down in the corners, lessening his appeal. Makes him more formidable, though, so I guess it's worth it to him.

"I'm glad to hear you say that Elissa," he stated mildly.

Now that he had turned back into a professor, and his own property no longer hers, she felt free to criticize him. A very vain man, she thought. His work and his place on the pinnacle keep him inviolate. Fleetingly she remembered the young lecturer, his long neck with too much Adam's apple and his skinny wrists. Blushing for no reason. He could bend words to his will — as in time he taught her to do — but anything set him blushing. Meg's big brother. She hadn't given him a thought until she went to university and saw how, without doubt, he was marked out as the coming man. A thing girls love, their private possession of a public property. We all vied for him and I won. Does his life satisfy him, Elissa wondered. What's left for him to aim for? I think I know him inside out — but do I? There are areas where I never trespass.

"Come on, Elissa." He was irritable. "Get up, will you? If I get caught in the traffic I'll be stonkered." He had taken to using Australian slang. Stupid, it sounded. "Did I tell you to wear that grey dress tonight?"

"Oh yes, you told me. And I'll obey. I'll come swathed to the neck. To make up for your daughter's birthday suit. Shall I wear a yashmak?"

"Your daughter too," he reminded her.

She stretched. "Jim. Who said if I were crested not cloven, — or something like that — I'd outwarrior the world — or something."

"Queen Elizabeth," he answered, the repository of all wisdom. Suddenly he rounded on her, roaring. "Elissa, will you get up? And remember, I want you to put a good face on it tonight."

"Oh, I will. Don't I always?" She slid out of bed. "Tonight and tomorrow and forever after. Count on me."

3

Winter was over. Spring came and went, in fits and starts, offering soft airs then retreating behind savage showers. In the bushland, however, the new season was already well advanced. When Elissa glanced out of her car she saw sarsaparilla scrambling over stumps, and everywhere the fluffy yellow of Cootamundra wattle. The bulbuls had returned from wherever they'd gone. She stopped her car on the way back from the village shops beside the wide reserve that had once been part of Campbell land. She regarded it covetously. If I owned it now, all that slope of bush, I'd make it into a Paradise garden, Australian, of course, plants from here there and everywhere all over Australia. I'd coax them into growing, even if they didn't want to. Instead of that tangle of scrub ending in a muddle of sand and pampas grass, I'd make something pretty spectacular, like no bushland that ever was, with banksias as the background, growing as thickly as they did when the settlers first came and called the place Banksia Ridge. She wondered again, as she had wondered before, how much it would cost to buy it back again and who exactly it was that owned it now. The council, perhaps. She seemed to remember hearing Jim speak of his grandfather, usually so parsimonious (trust Jim to say parsimonious, not stingy) giving a great parcel of land to somebody or other in return, no doubt, for payment in kind. She had money, quite a lot of it. But to buy that land back now, with its four hundred feet to the road and its clear run down to the bay, you'd have to be a millionaire. No use eyeing it.

She started the car. Really one should be grateful that it hadn't been carved up into thirty allotments or more. Everything changes; even that, it's probably only a matter of time. Soon, they say, there'll be an airfield here, or hereabouts. Horrible thought. Air travel is becoming banal; no longer adventurous, merely sleazy. As so much has. And she thought, with satisfaction, of the land her own family had hung on to, over Faggotter's Beach. The Campbells owned hundreds of acres and now it's whittled down to a lousy one and a bit. But I still have what mama left me and no doubt Aunt Winifred will leave me hers. She'll have to, she's got nobody else. So if I — At the back of her mind something flickered and vanished. She tried to chase it: no good. But it will come back again, she told herself, wait. She started the car, turned first into her own street, then her own gateway.

Somebody was there before her. There, under an ironbark, ineptly parked, its bonnet touching the trunk, was Jeanie's old jalopy. For once, then, she had managed to come early. Mostly she came late and grubby. Today, Elissa noted, she was not only early, but almost clean. She ran appraising eyes over her daughter, standing, slouching more like it, in an apricot smock, nursing the ginger-haired baby, smiling at her two little girls, who had rounded the corner, whooping. Elissa got out of the car, eyeing them warily, as she always did. Where did they come from, those froggy popping eyes and wide froggy mouths? She wouldn't be surprised if they spoke in croaks.

"Early, Jean?" She bent to kiss them, Naomi first, then the little one, Miriamne. But Miriamne had escaped. Odd names, very. Kevin's idea, probably, and Jeanie went along with it. A born yes-woman. She pretended not to see that Naomi was rolling her eyes and poking out her tongue.

"Go and play leapfrog in the garden," she suggested. "I'll bring you out some lemonade soon. Don't tease Ka. And please, girls, don't push the swing against the conservatory."

"The glass house, darlings," Jeanie explained, when they looked stupefied. "Don't break the glass or you might get cut."

"Or even beheaded," said Elissa. They goggled and took off.

"Come along, Jean. I thought you were coming at twelve."

"Oh, I had to call in at school. I had to drop Rachel and the lamingtons. It's lamington day," she informed Elissa, full of virtue. "I made four dozen lamingtons for the lamington drive."

"And no doubt ate half a dozen along the way." Elissa noted the rich swell of breast and belly, the round curve of the rosy cheeks. "You're so pudgy, Jeanie. Why don't you try to get thinner? You're too young and — potentially — too pretty to be so much overweight."

The lustrous dark eyes glazed. Jeanie put on her mule face. "Kevin doesn't mind. And one baby after another doesn't give you time to get your figure back."

"Well, I hope you've stopped at four," said Elissa severely, leaning against the car and jingling the keys.

"Now I've got a boy I will. I s'pose you wish you'd kept on till you had one." Jeanie was in one of her impudent moods. She put her lips to the baby boy's scalp. She had him done up in plaid crawlers, although the poor child could hardly sit up. His fontanelle, beneath the smudge of red hair, was throbbing. He had cradle-cap.

Elissa smiled at the small hands reaching out, catching at leaves, missing them. "Not really," she answered, putting out her fingers for the baby to grasp. "Two girls were more than enough."

Jeanie wasn't listening. She took the baby's hand in hers and kissed the fingers, one by one. "Beautiful boy," she was whispering. "Clever little angel. He reaches for things so beautifully. He's got wonderful co-ordination. Boys are different," she added, looking up in triumph, proud of herself, oblivious of the dribble on the front of her dress.

Where did I get those girls, Elissa asked herself, quite distracted with annoyance, as she always was after a few minutes in Jean's company. One girl bent on playing the brood mare; the other a bawd, or close on. She saw that Jeanie was wearing health sandals, old and down at heel.

"Let's go inside," she said, leading the way to the house. Jeanie was so lymphatic that she would never move without prompting. "Where are those Italian sandals I gave you for your birthday, Jean?"

"Kevin says the heels are too high, I might trip over with Ab," said Jeanie, Kevin's virtuous spouse. "And they've never been the same since Miriamne threw them into the creek."

Miriamne. Their names got progressively fancier. Rachel. Naomi. Miriamne. And — horror of horrors — Absalom. Absalom O'Hara. Could affectation go further? The baby, who after all couldn't help his monstrous name, held out his arms to Elissa, and she took him from her daughter. His hair was the familiar Campbell red, but his face in every feature was hers: wide forehead, the slanted green eyes, the straight fine nose. The defined philtrum and the cleft chin, they were hers too. If I'd had a son, she thought, holding him to her, he would have looked like this one.

"He has his father's nose," Jeanie asserted. "It will be quite aquiline. I've got to get him down for his sleep now. I put his basket in your bedroom. Hope you don't mind."

Elissa went ahead to the kitchen. "I'll put on the kettle. No doubt you're famished."

Jean's greedy eyes fell on the almond biscuits, set out to cool, and on the crystallized violets, set out to dry. They moved then to the glass bowl massed with violets, long-stalked, the pinkish ends visible through the clear water.

"Cripes, our gardens are different," she remarked. "I bet it took you half an hour to pick those violets," she marvelled. "I bet you went out and picked them as soon as dad took off for Uni."

Elissa winced inwardly at the vulgarisms. Cripes. Uni. She did it on purpose, of course. Since she'd bedded down with the young pleb (as he called himself) with the alternative life-style (only work when you need bread) she'd adopted his vocabulary.

She's got no more personality than jelly-blubber, thought Elissa. Whatever Kev told her was law. Elissa was wary of Kevin, so fierce and so sensitive, a drop-out from university, turned carpenter. But then Jesus Christ was a carpenter, as Jeanie never failed to point out. They lived in a dump on the edge of the chase, with their own tract of bushland. Since they'd married Jean had become the patron saint of honest toil and nature triumphant. She hoarded and mouthed every word that fell from Kevin's sacred lips.

Jeanie took possession of her son again. "Kev's going to start work on landscaping next. He's really interested in natural gardens. Did I tell you, we're already keeping ourselves in vegies and fruit? And our chooks are marvellous layers."

Vegies. Chooks. "I'll get the girls some lemonade," said Elissa, opening the refrigerator. She always bottled the lemon drink that Jim liked; made lemon butter out of the bountiful crop from the lemon trees. Cumquat liqueur, marmalade, grape jam: each season in turn was sealed in glass. But surely it was unnecessary to crow about it. Look, she told herself, Jeanie's not my business now. Whatever she does with her life is up to her. She can ruin her figure and dress in rags, have four children or forty four — she's on her own. On her own with Kev. God, isn't this a horrible mess, she realized. Once she had it in for me. Now I've got it in for her. In silence she poured the drinks for the children.

"There's pea soup," she said, with an effort. "And caramel ice cream cake for the girls."

"Anything does us. We're not fussy," said her graceless daughter. "As long as it's healthy. Oh mama, haven't you given up smoking yet?"

"No. Not now or ever. I'm a lost cause." With some deliberation Elissa inhaled. She forestalled Jean as she flopped into a chair and began to unbutton her dress. "Please, Jean. If you intend to feed the baby will you go into the bedroom? This isn't a milking-shed."

Jean looked affronted. "God you're bourgeois!"

"Private. Not bourgeois, private. Some activities aren't meant for public gaze. And I don't want to hear what Kevin said!" cried Elissa, quite wildly, stubbing out her cigarette. She forced herself to speak quietly. "Did the white violets settle in?" On her last visit Jeanie had insisted on taking home clumps of white violets.

She was abashed. "Oh well actually Kev threw — I mean he gave them away. He wants our garden to be utterly natural. You can't imagine how subtle Australian wildflowers are, when you really look at them."

Quoting, she was quoting again. They had nothing to talk about, no common ground at all.

"Are you frightened out there?" Elissa was suddenly curious.
"What of?"

"Oh — bushfires. Snakes. Intruders."

"Not with Kevin. Here mum, take Ab. I'll go and give the girls their drinks before I feed him."

"Very quiet, aren't they?" The only sound from outside was the tiny beep-beep of the great crimson rosellas that haunted the garden. "When you and Jess were quiet it meant mischief."

"We weren't allowed to be mischievous. We were regimented every minute. When it wasn't ballet it was music and tennis and sailing. And fencing. Kev nearly passed out when I told him we had fencing lessons. We had no time to just *be*. I want my children to have time to —" She was silent.

"Blossom?" Elissa prompted. "Vegetate? Or just go to seed?"

"You really are a bitch!" said Jean, flushing. She jumped to her feet and dragged the baby out of Elissa's arms. "No wonder we hated you. You can't bear to share the limelight with anyone, can you? Keep your soup. I'm going home." At the door she turned. "Anyway whether you like it or not, Jess's got the star part now. So put that in your pipe and smoke it!"

Jean had taken off. Bundling her children into the car, leaving the baby's basket in the bedroom, replete with two dirty napkins and a discoloured clean one; together with a string of plastic teddy-bears and some torn mosquito netting. Elissa heard the car first refuse, then grudgingly consent to go. She was trembling.

So there it was, finally said. We hated you. It wasn't any news to her, really. She had always been aware of the antagonism in the two little girls: even as they stroked her furs and squirted themselves with her perfume, they were vying with her for their father's attention. He loved them, he tossed them up and teased them, but when Elissa beckoned, he put them down with a thump. Their voices still echoed in her head. Don't go, daddy. Tell us a story. Don't kiss mummy. But he always did go, and the stories remained half-finished.

Elissa went out into her garden, deeply disturbed, trying to find a calm centre in the whirlwind of her thoughts. That's one job I've made a hell of a muck of. I didn't know how to be a mother. Nineteen, twenty, I hadn't finished my turn of being a child. I loved them when they were babies, I think I did, yes, I know I did. She felt again the surge of possessive love that came when they were sick: their poor swollen mumpy faces, their bunged-up eyes and croaky voices when they had measles. Nothing was too much to do for them then. But once their babyhood was done and they showed themselves as female, it was — she sought to clarify her thoughts — it was a harem, and only one could rule. Yes, that was the trouble. So I ruled. And they hated me. Half loved, half hated me. If they'd been boys, they'd have been part of my court. She saw Jess at eight, all big teeth and freckles and knife-sharp glances. Whatever I suggested, she rebelled against it. And Jeanie, copy-cat, copying everything I did. Borrowing my airs, my sidelong glances, as she grew up, to catch herself a man. And having caught one, she uses him to flout me. See, I can do without you. Look at me, the Earth Mother. O Absalom, my son, my son. To hell with her, I need her less than she needs me. Which is not at all.

In the quiet of the walled-off garden, that a Victorian woman had fashioned, Elissa Campbell stood stock-still and looked within herself and looked backwards. I wish I had someone to talk to, she thought. Someone to show me the way to go, tell me what mistakes I've made and forgive me and show me how to put them right. There's no one I can turn to. They all think I'm invulnerable.

She thought of her mother, long-dead; so aloof, so exquisitely disdainful of the second-rate, such a — really, such a damned snob. Yet she could, when she chose, charm the birds off the trees. Was I jealous? No, not at all. I prized her and she prized me. These days, perhaps she'd take a lover, and I'd be left smouldering. And her girlish little partner would be an avowed queer. But in her era decorum was all. She saw her mother holding a tray of bread and honey for the lorikeets, the small dark head on the long column of neck. So unsparing of herself, so unyielding in her demand for perfection in herself and others. No wonder my father dallied with his little bits of fluff. No wonder she showed him the door. Elissa closed her eyes, the better to see her father, but no, his face escaped her. That was the key then, perhaps? We were never in competition ... The only thing I longed for was more of her company. The only thing I was jealous of was the work that kept her from me. I suppose, in the end, she was committed to her sense of beauty and decorum. And I — what am I committed to?

She felt again the sick shock that had stunned her when Jim told her that her mother was dead. Her car overturned on the way to decorate the church for somebody's wedding. The white camellias she carried, they cupped her blood and spilled over.

Why am I thinking all this? There's no help there. All she created, my mother, the house, the decorating business, it fell to pieces when she died. But I think, I'm sure she had reached her goal when she saw me married, and cosseted. I wish I could ask her what to do, how she felt when she had to take up cudgels at forty, or thereabouts. Sombre, Elissa scrutinized the sliver of white garden she had been allowed to make. She heard the pigeons roocooing, each to each in the branches of the handkerchief tree. White pigeons, white handkerchief tree: the conceit had pleased her. She reached out her toe, supple Italian leather, to Ka, lying at her feet, grabbing for her ankles with his dark paws. With one swift bound he rolled over and ran up the yulan. One more, and he was down, to frolic at her feet. His mother was buried under that tree. The years take away more than they give. She bit back tears.

4

Theo Kaufmann, who had changed with the years to Theodora Carmichael, gave a great big grin of welcome when she spotted Elissa. She was standing marooned in an almost-empty swimming pool, holding a bucket, up to her ankles in a puddle of green slime. Elsewhere the pool was uncannily clean, so huge and so white that it looked like a slab in a giant's mortuary. It's a behemoth, thought Elissa, it's disgusting.

"Come on in, the water's fine," called Theo, squinting upwards. "Hi." She was eighty feet away, at the deep end, dwarfed by the nine foot walls flanking her. Otto's last expansive gesture before he dropped dead; a pool he could stretch out in. She was a dwarf, anyway, hardly five feet tall, looking, because of her square build, even shorter. How grey she's grown, and her teeth have gone to rack and ruin. More than a bit deaf. Nice skin, though, Elissa allowed. She walked along the coping towards Theo, so that she wouldn't have to shout.

"Why don't you get your teeth capped, Ted?" She tempered the impertinence by using the old nickname.

"Why? What would I use for money? They're alright for chewing. The boys don't care. I don't care."

It was the truth. She didn't care how she looked as long as she functioned. She scrubbed up well, however. From time to time Elissa saw her, uneasily accoutred in the remnants of a rich wardrobe, sneaking in late to a party, or managing a stall at some local fete, a pretty, stocky woman in the thick of life. Mostly, though, doing a man's work in overalls or chlorine-stained shorts, she looked unspeakable, like something the cat had dragged in, then discarded.

"What in God's name are you doing down there?"

"I'm getting the pool ready for the summer season. Three gorgeous blokes like teddybears came and cleaned it out for me.

They left me with the debris and took off for the pub. I'll be with you in a sec. Go and sit down."

Elissa went back to sit at the wooden table that held a pile of books on modern swimming techniques, a Playboy, and a few empty beer cans. Theo came padding up to the shallow end, leaving a line of footprints to mark her trail.

"I was having an argument with the boss of the bears about Mark Spitz, you know, the butterflyer, how tall he is. I knew he was five feet ten. And he is! Gallagher said so!" cried Theo, in triumph, putting the bucket of muck on the pool side and climbing up after it. "I waited till after he left to check, though. I wouldn't want to offend him. I rely on him *utterly*." Theo picked up the bucket and went to empty it somewhere.

Left alone, Elissa looked round Theo's domain. It was a mess. The tennis court, across the lawn from the pool, was hemmed in by a wilderness of vivid blue morning glory, the wire sagging all whichways. Grass grew in the garden-beds. Crepe myrtles, unpruned and lanky, grew higher than trees. Coral trees made a thicket behind a stand of pittosporums. It had, if you wanted to be charitable, a certain ramshackle charm, but it was only one step removed from a jungle. Theo gardened by fits and starts. In the old days, when Otto was alive, she'd had the gardener plant a dozen magnolias, sixty gardenias, huge clumps of whatever else her whim dictated. Most had died. Some had flourished. The result was a fight to the death between the survivors. Two enormous soulangeanas and a cannibal beaumontia vine were currently locked in battle. An apricot oleander, fifteen improbable feet tall, waited its turn.

"Your garden is a mess," said Elissa, severely. "In all my life I've never seen one so utterly lacking in form."

Back in the pool, now wading in slush, now padding up with another bucketful, Theo nodded agreement. "I know," she said, equally. "Like my life. Like me. Shapeless."

Her comical expression, sham-humble, made Elissa laugh. Theo laughed too and left her labours to come and sit on the grass at Elissa's feet. "How d'you always manage to look so absolutely bloody beautiful?" she enquired, not a tinge of envy in her curiosity. "There's not a line on your face. Your neck's as marvellous as ever. And you haven't even got one grey hair." She ran dirty hands through her own thick grey crop.

"Oh, I give it a rinse sometimes." Already Elissa felt better, as one always did with Theo. The trouble was, you could never get hold of her. Those boys owned her, body and soul. Something in her matter-of-fact cheerfulness always rubbed off on Elissa. I wish I knew her secret, she thought, gazing at the square face, the clear eyes as pale as aquamarines, the fanned-out lines deepening as Theo smiled at her.

"Want a drink? Though actually I haven't got any grog in the house." She followed Elissa's gaze to her feet, flat and dirty, with cracked soles. "Hideous, aren't they? Never mind, they get me along. If you were a true friend you'd get into overalls and pig in. Some chance," she finished. "Elissa, hurry up and tell me what you want. I've got to get this finished soon, so I can start filling it again. Otherwise the cement might crack and we won't eat."

"I came for — really, I came for comfort. And advice," Elissa said slowly, her words falling into a silence, spattered only with bird-calls. "What makes you so happy, Ted?" She looked into the glass of Theo's eyes. "I've got myself in such a state, I don't know how to be happy any more."

"Oh." Theo fished out a bee that had landed in the bucket. "Buzz off, stupid. Look, I don't know. Am I happy? I suppose I am. I don't really have time to think, I'm so busy cooking and cleaning up and teaching and scraping to pay the bills." She scratched her nose, started to pick it, then stopped. "Pray God I don't get sun-blisters on my lips this year. When that happens I'm anything but happy."

"How do you feel about it?" Elissa persisted. "Teaching the rabble?"

"Oh, that's going a bit far, don't be such a snob. They're beaut, nearly all of them. The kids are beaut and most of the mothers are very nice. I feel like a harlot when I hold out my hand for the money." She gave her grin, so well-remembered. Theo on Speech Day, mimicking some pompous visitor. "Just as well we've got the bloody pool, I'd never earn a crust on my back. Have a look at the Playboy the men left behind, you've got no idea of the competition. You'd be alright."

"Thank you," Elissa murmured.

"What was I saying, oh, money. Well, if I'm to get the boys launched, I've got to hold out my hand."

Elissa spoke with sudden fury. "I suppose you know it's all for nothing. They'll be done with you in a few years. It won't last forever."

Theo shrugged. "What does? By then I'll be glad of a rest, probably. Wasn't it Shaw who said that the crown of life is to be used up by a great purpose, then chucked aside. Something like that. Ask Jim, he'd know."

"Oh, Jim." Elissa was scornful.

"You're too damn cavalier with Jim. One day you'll go too far."

Elissa did not answer. She was watching Theo's bitser dogs haring around the shrubbery, rolling over, flattening the plants. No wonder the place looked a shambles.

Theo answered the unspoken criticism. "Life's too short to worry. The garden's for us, not the other way round." She waited for Elissa to speak. "Go on," she prompted, at last. "Finish what you were saying."

"I don't know what's wrong with me. I'm wretched." Elissa tried to smile, but tears ran down her cheeks. "Absurd, isn't it?"

"Is it the menopause? Early?"

"No, I don't think so. No indications at all. I just feel so purposeless. I'm sick to death of the round. I can't stand the luncheons and committees and golf and faculty dinners. I went to one the other night and I wanted to scream. And there's another one coming up."

"What about your girls? What do they say?"

"Well, Jess is fully occupied, as you know. And Jean and I don't get on. We don't speak the same language."

"She was always resentful of you, of course," said Theo, in her down-to-earth way. "I should think Jess might be able —"

"Theo, I'm desperate. Now I'm the one who's jealous. I'm jealous of both of them. I'm jealous of you. I'm jealous of anyone who's happy. I hate myself, but I can't stop. I don't know where to go from here."

Theo was troubled. "You were too young getting married. I was so old I was grateful. Everything was a bonus. You could try being grateful," she suggested, staring up the pool's length, watching the boys' imbecile pet hen as it scratched under a daphne bush, then took off.

"For what?"

"Oh, everything. Well, Jim, for one. I always had my eye on Jim. When I was growing up I used to pray he'd fancy me. I hated you for snaffling him."

"Really?" Life was full of revelations. "I hardly knew he existed till I went to university and saw the other girls eyeing him. I thought he looked like a stork."

"You never finished your course. Why don't you go back to university?"

"Why?"

"Learn a language?"

"I know four. Three too many."

"Well then, charity work. And there's your lovely garden. You've got too much time on your hands." Theo was suddenly angry.

"Oh Theo, the garden's finished. It doesn't have to be created, only maintained. And look, I do think Bertha's marvellous, but I can't see the point in feeding crippled babies. Life's hard enough when you've got all your senses."

Theo interrupted her, quite roughly. "Could be you're spoiled rotten."

"Yes, I am. That's the whole point. I don't have to earn

money. I wish I had sons, but I haven't got any. If I'm not needed for anything, then I want to distinguish myself. I feel a flop. Look, Jim's got his work and the girls have got their lives. And I've got nothing."

"Only beauty. Charm. Taste. Money." Inexorably, Theo ticked them off on her fingers, that ended in broken nails.

"I want to do something *spectacular*!" Elissa cried desperately.

"Go and hang yourself from the harbour bridge. In flames." Theo was cold. "And stop moaning, eh?" She looked down at the blisters on her ugly hands, opened her mouth, then closed it.

"Please Theo darling, don't be horrible. I know it's all piffling, but please try to help me. Please Teddy, you know you're on velvet —" Tears splashed on to her hand. "I haven't cried for years, and now I've cried twice in an hour. It's mad but I can't help it. You're good at coping. Teach me how. Or I'll take to the bottle or teenage lovers to fill in my days."

Theo sighed. The coldness left her eyes. "You're very good at decorating. You could open a shop, like your mother."

"Yes. Ye — es. Oh, I don't know ... I'd hate hustling for money."

"Do it free."

"Then I'd feel cheated."

"Garden planning, then. Why don't you really learn about garden design? Go to — oh wherever they teach it. The institute or tech or whatever it's called. Do it properly."

It was a possibility. Elissa considered the notion. "What would I do with it once I had my degree. Or diploma, if that's what it is."

"Simple." Theo made a gesture, sketching circles in air. "Design gardens. For people. Improve the suburbs. And give the money away, if you don't want it. To people who need it."

"You said you don't like taking money."

"I'd like it less if I didn't. Boys' shoes and school uniforms, they cost the earth." She got up with surprising swiftness for one so bulky. "I can't think of anything else, Elissa. I've got to get on with the job." From the pool floor she looked up. "You've got the prettiest legs," she said. "Like Vivien Leigh. She was one of your mob. Too damn lovely for her own good. I'll lend you her biography, if you like."

"Thank you, no thank you." Elissa flicked open the book she had brought to lend to Theodora, The Great Gardens of Australia. Misleading title, not one of them achieved greatness, except perhaps the Pioneer Mill, the only one with real scale. As for Eryldene, my garden is far more beautiful, and there's no way I'd call it great. I'd like to make a really great garden, she thought, excitement washing over her. Not one merely charming, or captivating; but one where every single part was subordinate to a single great end. I could, I know I could. She caught her breath.

A frenzy of barking, mixed with shouts. The two dogs were running in circles. Two boys, two striplings, were chasing them, or being chased in and out of the jacarandas. Elissa looked them over. One — Jeremy? — was still a child, fair and skinny. But the other one — Jonny — was halfway to manhood, a dark line of moustache above his beautiful sensual mouth. He stopped short, startled, and measured her with round eyes the colour of honey, a smile starting in them, mysteriously, then travelling to his lips. There was a bead of saliva on his lower lip, as pristine and clear as dew on a rose-leaf. He said nothing, but stood smiling at her.

"Hi, mum," called Jeremy, in a child's voice.

"You know Elissa, boys," came a voice from the depths of the white cavern. "We went to school together."

"Together? You and mum?" The dark boy, Jon, looked at her in disbelief.

"Appearances to the contrary," called Theo.

The boy turned to his mother, looking down at her with the same expression of amused tenderness. Women will be crazy for him, thought Elissa. His voice had deepened, but his words, when he spoke, were a schoolboy's.

"Mum's the missing link. I reckon we'd make our fortune if we sold her to a laboratory. Don't do any more work mum, I'll fix it up for you in a minute."

Elissa stood up slowly, stretching. "You're taller than I am, Jon. You've grown up overnight."

Boisterous, clued-up, Theo pulled herself out of the pool and stood between them. "He's fourteen," she said firmly. "Boys, there's a chocolate cake inside. Don't eat it all. And get changed first." She watched as they ran off, scuffling. Then she turned to Elissa. "Better stick to gardens, Liss. Not the bottle or the other thing."

5

James was nettled about the marmalade. To please him, each year Elissa made a thinly-sliced lemon marmalade, acid rather than bitter. Alas, it was all used up. The replacement she offered him, from Fortnum and Mason's, was not to his taste. In the whole world, it seemed, there was nothing he wanted so much as what he couldn't have.

"Like that nauseating king in the Cwistopher Wobin book. Only it was butter he wanted," she mused aloud.

"Ha ha," he said mirthlessly. "Very funny."

For a public personage, a man respected, probably honoured in his field, he could be quite surprisingly childish, en famille. Tonight, however, he would be on display: taller than anyone else in the room, intelligent, unflappable.

She let him rave on. But after a while she judged that enough was enough, and sought for a means of attack, in order to sidetrack him. "So why do I always have to go?" she interrupted. "Forget the jam. I've got injuries too. Why have I always got to turn up at these dreary dinners."

"Wives do," he answered shortly.

"I'm wives, am I?"

He made no response, but began to swallow his coffee in big gulps. The issue of the marmalade no longer had any importance for him. The last thing in the world he wanted, as she well knew, was a wrangle before a ceremonial occasion; she had often used the knowledge to wrest a minor victory.

"It'd be a pretty frowsy affair without you, Elissa," he said punctiliously. Also advisedly. Because really, for two pins or less she'd refuse to go. He wiped his mouth with his napkin. There was a smear of egg on his chin.

"Egg on your face. Chin." She pointed to the spot.

"Out damned —" he started to say, then stopped, perhaps remembering how she hated academic jokes. "They rely on you for a touch of beauty. And sex. And —" he had to gild the lily, to mock her, putting all his compliments in jeopardy. He was a pretty good adversary. " — And, of course, wit." He pushed back his chair and came to kiss the top of her head, in parting. "Look, um, seductive, will you? While maintaining discretion. We need to put best foot forward."

"Don't I always?" said Elissa, bored stiff in advance.

The union rooms were, as usual, the scene. Someone had perpetrated an astonishing arrangement of lilac and delphiniums and plastic November lilies; wired to a ramrod stiffness, they were displayed on all available dark wood surfaces. Despite the plethora of lights, the room looked dingy. Elissa, entering with Jim, ran practised eyes over the gathering. The mixture as before, unfailingly. Half a dozen senior staff members, with their ladies, were assembled here in the ante-room, toying with their (she knew in advance) dismal sherries. She could tell without looking what the women would be wearing, how their hair would be done, how the conversation, stiff at first, would get a jerky move on, and at last begin to flow. Like the tomato sauce bottle tipped up at the picnic: first none'll come and then a lot'll. Diana Drew — Professor Drew — not in the least modish, but possessed of great style, signalled a preoccupied greeting. Her coil of brown hair was coming loose from its pins. She was giving a mini-lecture on — Elissa craned — the subject of antic rice in modern literature. Oh, anti-Christ. Her thin, clever face, illumined by thought, turned to first one, then another of her audience for acquiescence. She's too sallow for black, though, decided Elissa, unless she slaps on the rouge. No chance of that. Jim, who admired her, went to join her court. Three men took advantage of his coming to escape to Elissa's side. Two of them made port. The third, Phil Jenkins, was intercepted by his wife, a neat outflanking movement. Sulkily he went to get her a sherry.

Four men, in a half-circle, stood mooning at Elissa. In red silk (seductive), long-sleeved (discreet), she turned the green spotlight of her gaze on them, smiling with lips and eyes, accepting their homage. Guy. Francis. Donald. Robby. All of an age, two of them bald, two still hanging on to their topknots. Academic quips. University accents. Robby was puffy under the eyes.

"What sort of celebration left you feeling like that, Robby?"

"My divorce. I was celebrating my third sortie into freedom."

"Once you'd have been turfed out," said Guy, in his namby-pamby voice. "Think of Christopher Brennan. Think of poor old Piggot."

"Thank God for more enlightened times." At forty something Robby still had acne, but, in compensation, a good lick of boyish charm.

"Really, Elissa, the girls besiege us," complained Donald, red-faced and bald as an ostrich egg. "They'd rather ape the Grand Horizontals than apply themselves to their Anglo-Saxon."

Elissa shrugged. "Girls haven't changed much. Only their approach. But tell me, Donald, why are we bidden here? Jim was vague. Or perhaps I wasn't paying attention."

"Dearly beloved, we are gathered here to welcome a prestigious American professor who is to give us a series of lectures on the advantages of obscenity. America's contribution to twentieth century literature. He is connected with a very impressive foundation."

Her attention wavered. Ada, Donald's wife, was up to her third sherry, and impassioned. She held Guy's wife captive. Her voice sliced clean across the spaces between. "I held it in my hand and I assure you it was like cardboard. How could anyone sit on the thing, I asked him. It's a sign of decadence, to offer it for sale."

"What are you on about, Ada?" called Elissa. "What's a sign of decadence?"

"Lavatory seats." Ada looked surprised. "Plastic no thicker than an egg-shell."

"Insupportable," breathed Elissa. Not a good joke, not even

precise. However, the men guffawed.

"Now Elissa, you're not to accuse Ada of harbouring a cloacal obsession," said Donald. "Nor me. My fetish, if I have one, lies in the near vicinity."

Elissa laughed. Oh God, she thought, I can't stick much more of this. She turned to Guy. It was clear that he too had had enough of Donald. "What's his subject, your visiting Vip? I haven't done my homework."

"The Jewish element in post-war American literature."

Jim loped over, Doug Denham by his side, a gooped-up brandy in his hand. "Here you are, Elissa. I told you the drinks were going to be better. I had a look at the wine list, too. You might be surprised. Oh Donald, I haven't had a chance to tell you how much I liked your slant on Furphy. It opened up one or two fascinating possibilities."

Elissa stifled a yawn. Far off, she heard Diana Drew's voice, light, even and penetrating. "On the contrary," she was declaring. Then her voice grew softer, dropped out of range.

"Come over to the embrasure, my dear Elissa," begged Guy, his toupee askew, his eyes bright, although red-rimmed. He was a notable gossip. "I've been longing to get you alone for months. I was laid low at the last shindig. Tell me about Jessica's — uh —" He sought for a word.

"Escapade? Peccadillo?" she prompted.

"Lapse," he said, pretending gravity. "Every syllable. I'm agog."

Elissa looked into the wry monkey face, began to bridle, then thought better of it. "Oh Guy, it was loathsome. The papers blew it up and that made it worse."

"Of course." Guy's face was alight with mischief, or perhaps malice. "Jim was imperturbable."

"It rocked him, though. Both of us. Sappho's Daughter —" She made a gesture of pushing it away. "It's rubbish, the worst kind of rubbish. Muck set to music. It's — oh — Jessica plays the daughter in love with both her mother and a young stud.

Naked. I'm ashamed of her."

"Anyone for incest?" murmured Guy. "In the manner of the times, though. What would you have her do? Hole up in repertory for years? Effrontery's of the essence now."

"It's worse than the casting-couch. Everyone who buys a ticket owns her. So —"

"What are you, Elissa?" Guy interrupted. "Affronted? Or envious?"

She swung on him. "What makes you say that?"

"You're circumscribed in your efforts, Eliza. Infinite riches in a little room." He gestured towards the gathering. "Perhaps you should have been a Buff Orpington."

Elissa was rigid with anger. "I'm quite aware what a Buff Orpington is, Guy. So don't waste your academic sarcasm on me. Nor on Jessica." Her voice was high, higher than she'd intended. Betty Denham halted, pricked up her ears, then in her well-bred way resumed her own conversation.

"My dear Eliza," Guy begged. "Don't be angry. My point was that the fair Jessica can't hold a candle to her mama. Now if it were you up there, au naturelle, I should be off on the first flight."

"The first cheap flight," Elissa amended.

"Oh yes, cheap, of course, that's the operative word... It's the age of the superficial. And the cheap. But if I said envious, it was because I find myself in that boat." His eyes were swivelling. It occurred to Elissa that he was a sick man, not far from cracking. He went on. "Did I tell you that my son David has taken up deep-sea diving? Could anything show more plainly what he thinks of his father's profession?"

"It's dangerous, I suppose?" asked Elissa, when the silence showed that he needed an answer.

"Very. Outlandishly dangerous. Really a most bizarre choice. I confess I'd be petrified. So — am I proud? Or am I consumed with envy? Who can tell? In my crass way I assumed that you, too — But perhaps you're glad to have no part of it?"

Glad, am I glad? Or am I glad to be part of this cerebral setup? Not that I'm part of it at all, I'm just on the fringe. Before she could sort out her thoughts, she heard the tempo of conversation change.

"The iceman cometh," whispered Jim, taking her elbow to guide her towards the newcomer, a burly brown fellow with short legs, a quantity of beard, and, surprisingly, kilts. The Cameron tartan. Suddenly she was sick of being a lady, of always, always doing the indicated thing. She shook Jim off. Just for once she wanted to drop a clanger. And she would.

"Why does an American wear the Cameron tartan?" she asked, selecting a brilliant smile, moving towards him.

"Because he's a Cameron, dyed in the wool," he answered, in the Southern drawl that Jim had told her approximated Shakespeare's own speech.

"I was a Cameron too. Before I became a Campbell. But although I am of Scottish descent, one question has never been answered."

"What is that?" He leaned towards her, short-legged as a Corgi, smelling of lifesavers, his dark eyes twinkling.

"What do Scotsmen wear under their sporrans?" she asked, very gravely. Beside her, Jim was stiff with chagrin. She didn't care at all. She tilted her head, and waited for the answer.

Cameron (Professor? Doctor? Emperor?) threw back his head and laughed. A good lusty laugh he had there. "I shall be delighted to arrange a demonstration," he promised. And the room, no longer craning to hear, rocked with relieved academic laughter.

6

The hill was infinitely more beautiful than she had remembered. All else had changed. With the widening of the road, the traffic now shuttled ceaselessly, as never-stopping as the ocean, that was hidden and silenced by the great sugarloaf hill. The noise was execrable. Remembering the days when the coastal road was little more than a track, when the land around Faggotter's Beach spilled into paddocks or tumbled green to the bay, Elissa was grieved.

In the days when she had lived with her mother on the tuft of level ground, halfway to the top, she had never thought much about the beauty of the bushland, nor taken time to contemplate the magnificence of the final view that waited at the crest. Mostly she was injured because she had to ride her bike a mile and a half to school. All the action was at Banksia Ridge. By comparison, even Hammerhead, there to the north, was a hamlet.

Now it was all different. The dairy was a thicket of small plots and big houses. A dozen or more estate agents chaffered in Hammerhead township, which had quite lost the seedy charm it once possessed. The rather magical thing about the hill, however, was its western side, where it hung poised above village and bay, and the dark green hump of the chase beyond the bay ... Here, on the west, the hill had been split into only three holdings: the lie of the land had made subdivision impossible. And the other side fell sheer to the sea, to the beach called Faggotter's, who knows why, frequented only by those in the know. As a child she had swum there. Children still rode their ponies across the sand.

Elissa parked the car in the cursory space allotted, on the cracked cement overgrown with dandelions, and began the long climb up the rickety stairs to the house she had left twenty five years back; where her Aunt Winifred was domiciled now, at least until the walls caved in and the roof collapsed on her.

She toiled upwards. An enormous dead angophora, which divided her aunt's land from her mother's house (mine, really, she thought) was filled with kookaburras, in corroboree. The noise made her shake her head: a dozen kookaburras in spate, it's too much of a good thing. A blue-tongue opened a sudden mouth at her feet, almost catapulting her down the stairs. They were slippery with moss and maidenhair fern, edged with native violets. Halfway up to the house she took a breather; even in flat shoes it was a stiff climb. The noise of the road was muffled here, and the road itself out of sight. The waving branches of box and gum and turpentine masked the toy trucks and cars, reduced them to a sound no louder than a beehive, although more spasmodic. Down in the valley below there was almost no sign of habitation, for the same reason, she surmised, that there was nothing much up here: a terrain that made roads impossible. She was pricked by sudden memory — oh, of course, the Generalife, with its gruelling climb to the mirador. At the back of her mind something clicked and vanished. She turned her attention to the scene before her and below and beyond. She took in the sweep, or rather plunge of olive-green and black-green, where pittosporums and banksias and gums struggled and locked branches, and the gold of the last pycnantha wattles shone strident. Beyond the valley stretched the bay, transparent, ice-blue, cut by long spurs of indigo deep water and by the dull-yellow tongue of the sand-bar. It's silted up, she thought, I'm sure it used to be deeper. She was annoyed at the cluster of boats moored here and there, a great clot of them at the marina. Very plebeian, boating, these days, like so much else. The great levelling, as Guy put it. The triumph of the plebs, as Kevin put it. And went on to say, reasonably enough, why shouldn't we triumph? Why not, she thought, and she shrugged.

However, there is a certain satisfaction to be got from standing knee-deep in wildflowers on your own land, no other dwelling within cooee, and just out of cooee the falling-down humpy of the old farmer and his half-crazed wife. Though how he could farm anything up here, she couldn't imagine. Was he still alive? I must ask Aunt Winifred, she thought. Don't go up that way, my mother used to say, they're strange people, fee fi foh fum. So I didn't.

Elissa shivered; the breeze was cold. She began again to climb. Self-sown passionfruit almost tripped her up. She stooped and picked one, unexpectedly purple among its green neighbours. A loquat tree straddled the path, no, two trees entwined. The roots had almost displaced one of the steps. She caught at a branch for support as Kylie, the kelpie, flew out of nowhere showing her teeth and barking, then retreating to the landing of the stairs, to redouble her efforts. Her black fur was a ruff around her neck.

"Hello, Kylie." Elissa knew it was all sham. She patted the dog. She must be seven or eight, but showed no sign of age, still shiny and limber, leaping ahead to announce the newcomer.

The terrace, with its little garden of pinks and cherry-pie and forget-me-nots, was strewn with blown leaves and twigs; it was dishevelled and unused. Aunt Winifred was in bed. Very frail she looked, her skin stretched waxen across the bones; her eyes, however, bright and darting. She had on a blue cashmere nightgown, with cocoa spilled down the front. Her thin, blue-veined hand flew up to cover the stain. Her white hair, usually so shiny, had no lustre.

"You didn't tell me you were ill," Elissa accused her. Most days, although not unfailingly, she made the gesture of a quick telephone call to her mother's aunt: all that remained of family.

"I didn't want to worry you, darling." Aunt Winifred's eyes grew moist with tears. Unmarried, childless, with no one else to dote on. It was a bit of a bind, all that weight of affection.

"What's wrong?" Elissa perched on the patchwork quilt, laboriously and unskilfully worked by her aunt, fifty years back.

"It's my heart, darling, that's all. A thing that happens to old ladies," said the little voice like a cracked bell. "I know what I have to do. I take to my bed until I feel able to take charge of things again. Kylie looks after me." Kylie, hearing her name, wagged her tail. "There's nothing that can't be left until I feel able to cope. That's one of the advantages of being old."

That was true: nothing much to look after. There were only four rooms, made of stout timber, unpainted inside and out, weathered by now to an exquisite grey, some timber that was supposed to last forever. The floor, she remembered, was tallow wood; she remembered helping her mother to sand it smooth, oil it golden. Not much furniture, but what there was, old stuff and good. She crossed to the windows and looked out, across the shallow terrace, where the pale pink and green leaves were bursting out of the grape buds.

"Your grape's earlier than mine," she remarked. She thought of her mother twisting up the tendrils. She saw her standing at this window, looking at herself in her heavy gold looking-glass, turning her head to see the back of her new shingle, directing the reflection from one glass to another. So comely in all her movements. She felt tears prickle her eyes. I was at the start of life then, I hadn't buggered it all up.

"Darling girl, are you crying? I'm alright, I told you," said Aunt Win, leaning forward, sending out a dry smell of lavender and baby powder and old age. "Kylie looks after me, don't you, girl?" From the floor Kylie thumped acknowledgement.

"How life flies," said the old lady. "If Kylie's mother were alive she'd be fifteen. It was all such a mystery. I'd never had her spayed. None of the male dogs ever found their way up —"

"Like a princess in a tower," said Elissa, lighting up. She had heard this story before.

"And when she was eight, she had one puppy, Kylie. It was a mystery. I never saw a sign of a male dog, then or since."

"Like the Holy Ghost."

"Don't be blasphemous, dear. Or flippant." Aunt Winifred sighed. "When she died, I was very glad to have little Kylie. But I had the vet fix Kylie up."

"Times have changed. Girls are more promiscuous now," said

62

Elissa, bored.

"Now, Elissa, don't make fun of me. But I confess, dear, I do worry about what's going to happen to her when I die." She put a bookmark inside A Farewell to Arms, which was open on the bed beside her. She closed it, firmly, looked down at the cover, then raised her eyes to Elissa's. "For of course dear, I can't live forever. I'm eighty four. I can't bear the thought of her looking for me and — I was too old to take her mother, but then of course I had no choice. She was whimpering by the door in the rain — Another mystery." She sank back, deep in her memories.

"Oh Aunt Winifred, put your mind at rest. I'll take her if the question arises. I'll see that she's happy. I promise you." Elissa, meaning to stop there, was amazed to hear herself plunge on, words spilling from her lips, framing thoughts she hadn't known she harboured. "Aunt Win, do something for me, will you?"

"Darling, anything you want."

"You've left me the land, your land next door, haven't you? Please, can I have it now?"

The old eyes questioned. She waited while Elissa stubbed out her cigarette. "Why, Elissa?"

"Aunt Win, I don't know why. I think I want to —" As she spoke, it became clearer to her, the hazy picture in her mind. "I want to put the two blocks together, to start to plan a —" She saw her aunt's expression, austere; and she lied. "To make a — it sounds mad — a sort of memorial to mama — A great garden —" She faltered into silence. To distort the truth for her own ends, to offer that mixture of truth and lies to one so loving and so gullible, oh, how low can you get?

Her aunt's cracked lips, the colour of the underside of a mushroom, parted over her new false teeth in a sentimental smile. "Darling, what a beautiful idea. Of course. Do you want to start it now?"

"Aunt Winifred, I don't know what I want, really," answered Elissa, quite ashamed of herself. To manipulate an old and besotted relative, it was a pretty poor show. But she had to go on. "I think I've been turning it over in my mind without realizing what I was doing. It would be very exciting to plan a big garden from beginning to end. I've never had the chance. But I'd like to get started now, I think." She bent her head.

"Of course, pet." She heard the old, faraway voice. "I fear I'm not long for this world, anyway. Would you name it after Stella?"

But Elissa put her head down on the quilt that smelled of moth balls and dead roses and felt the bones of the spindly old legs beneath. Something in the old woman's unquestioning goodness made her despise her own manipulations. But then, she had taken herself by surprise too. "Aunt Win, I don't really know myself what I mean, it's all hazy. I've been looking for a purpose in life. To make a really wonderful garden, right from scratch, that might be the answer."

"Your mother would expect me to give you anything you asked for." She reached out and patted Elissa's hand. "Your skin is so soft, darling. You're so like her. How pleased she was when you married James. Life is so strange," said the old lady, looking backwards, hooded old eyes with crepy lids. "She was almost a Campbell herself, you know. She was much in love with James's father, and he with her. But he married money. Oh, she was heartbroken, poor child. I'll never forget her face when she heard the news." Elissa was taken aback, very. All this in the past, and not one word said before this. She listened. "It almost broke her heart. She married on the rebound, you know. It seldom works," said this maiden lady, who had brought up Elissa's mother. "Oh dear, it was a sad business. He tried to begin an affaire with her, James's father, after James was born. But your mother showed him the door, I'm glad to say."

Elissa was, by now, flabbergasted. What a close-mouthed lot I come from. Does Jim know? I think not. "It's practically incestuous," she said at last, hearing her voice quaver. Then again, one didn't have to put on a front with Aunt Win. "No wonder I feel stifled. I'm practically married to my own brother.

Aunt Win, you're awfully skinny, your poor little legs are just skin and bone. I'll go and see what I can find to cook you. Would you like an omelette?" She pulled off her silk dress, slipped off her shoes, peeled off her pantyhose. Barefoot, in her petticoat, she padded to the kitchen, and put on the big, old-fashioned apron she found hanging behind the door. "I'll get the kitchen scrubbed out, too. Kylie's been dragging her food round the floor. And I'll take your washing home. Really, you know, you shouldn't be living all by yourself."

"You're a good girl, darling," said her aunt, misty-eyed, and oh God, manipulated. "I'll telephone Mr Moffitt and tell him to make the land over to you. After all I'm living in your house — and you've never breathed a word. You could have turned me out and pocketed the money."

Don't put thoughts into my head, begged Elissa, silently. I'm scheming enough already, without being encouraged. Aloud she said demurely, good little, pretty little, ten year old Elissa. "Thank you, Aunt Winifred."

7

At night now she lay awake in a blissful daze, half-dreaming, as she had lain, becalmed, in the happiest time of her life, that trip abroad, with the children safely dispatched, Aunt Winifred as resident guardian; and James, who had strayed (perhaps not too far) returned to her and content, like the warrior returned to his Ithaca. And all Europe that she had longed to really see, to take time to see, unfolding itself to her. All the promises coming true. The gallantry of the French. The undisguised admiration of the Italians, who didn't dare to pinch her black and blue, as they had pinched that lying Rhonda — or was it Frances? — because James was there, always in surveillance. That blissful time, when all life seemed to be opening up and full of promise, as if she could have anything in the world she wanted: all hers for the taking. Thirteen years back, or fourteen. A long time, anyway.

Her thoughts these days were rueful, not aggrieved. For each spring day, sun-warmed, each star-peppered night, her mind returned again and again to her scheme, unrealized, indeed, only half-glimpsed. And what if she did make a garden — what would she do with it? And what sort of a garden exists unless to embellish a house? A park, of course. But it wasn't a park, or a public garden that she envisaged. James, though, he'd never leave Rosencrantz. Rosencrantz: a stupid name. Once she had thought it beautiful. At that point her thoughts always veered off; lost themselves in the heady and imprecise excitement of creation before it is grindingly begun. Not the time to make obstacles, or you'd never get started.

What she had to do first, before anything, was to get hold of the rest of the land, so that she owned all the west side of the hill. And she would. She reiterated the down-to-the-bone dialogue of marriage (bed-springs, not violins, for accompaniment) expertly amorous, seemingly involved; but for all that, absent-minded. One night Jim, depositing the expected kiss, missed her lips and found, instead, her eyelids; he was surprised to find them wet with tears. Lately, nonsensically, she was always on the verge.

"Elissa. What's wrong?" He leaned over her, "Did I hurt you?"

Arrogant bugger, so certain of his brute strength. She blinked and began to laugh. "Sorry to disappoint you, Samson. It was just — an old song came into my head suddenly, I don't know why. Kisses sweeter than wine."

He remembered it, one of their songs. He was almost tone-deaf: music played little part in his life. But this song he recalled, because the gondolier had sung it. In Italian. It was having a revival, that year.

"No need to weep," he told her, very smug, very lordly. "Even for happiness." Then he made amends and echoed the words of the song. "I'd do it again too. I think."

Now was the moment to put it to the test. She had pored over the plans of her aunt's land (soon to be hers) and of her mother's land (already hers). Now if only she had the block next door —

"James. Dearest," she whispered, holding him with thongs of silken flesh. "Don't go. Be sociable. Darling, are you rich?"

"Moderately," he answered. "Why?"

"Would you give me some money if I asked you?"

He wasn't too sure, stingy bugger. "If necessary," he said, with the true-blue Campbell caution. "How much?"

"Oh — about forty thousand dollars. Or a bit less. For a whim."

He exploded, taking off like a cork out of a bottle. "Certainly not," he stated, turning his back on her. "You've got a queer sense of humour, Elissa."

Recriminations were not in order; nor was further wheedling. Right, then, she'd manage without him. Her tears (sentimental? — or merely manipulative?) were, hey presto, dried. I don't care, she thought, staring mutinous into the darkness, I don't need you anyway, you skinflint. I can borrow on mama's house. And all those bonds I've never bothered about, they'd be worth a lot by now. So you can't stop me. If I told you, you'd hit the roof, no wonder we've lasted, I've never opposed you, hardly ever.

She heard him snuffling into the pillow, getting ready for the first snore of the night.

At the Garden Club, where she'd been summoned by an S.O.S. from Bertha, laid low with shingles, and so unable to man the coffee machine — there in the stone building where they held their meetings, Elissa dallied with her pleasant thoughts. She rarely put in an appearance here. Their activities seemed to her circumscribed; she preferred her work with the National Trust. But a call from Bertha was not to be denied. She sat among the ladies, seemingly attentive, aware of herself as someone she hardly knew, languorously happy: like being in love. While Lady Armitage, the guest speaker, showed her slides and her bonsais, and told her stories of the small symbolic gardens of Japan, while she spoke of prostrate and recumbent and stones and bridges, Elissa Campbell's thoughts roamed free over a wider territory. Say then the old man was willing to sell. He might be, his wife was dead, he had one foot in the grave and the other on a banana skin, said Joe, her gardener. And Joe would know: long time resident of Hammerhead, on speaking terms with all the old relics, storehouse of old scandals and secrets. What Joe said wouldn't be far wrong. Bright's disease, failing fast, said Joe. A terrible dirty old coot, always drives a hard bargain. Joe remembered, with embellishments, the time he'd helped to quarry out stone so the old bloke could make a vegetable garden. Sixpence, he paid me. Can I have a bit of the stone to sell? Get off, or I'll tan the arse off you. Chased me off his land, he did, Joe remembered. He's a hermit, like. They say he's got to sell up and go in on the kidney machine.

Elissa, sitting still, listening as one rapt, with Rhonda on one side, Helen on the other, busied herself with what she'd learned from Joe, come to carry out his weekly stint. This morning, just before she came here, when she took him out his bottle of beer and his money. A profitable morning, she thought. And I'll go up and beard the old man tomorrow, I won't wait. She put her hands together, slightly hollowed, to produce a more enthusiastic handclap. The meeting, which had coincided with a fashion parade, was not well attended.

In the small room behind the main hall, the urn was almost boiling. She set out cups and saucers, sliced date loaf thinly, filled serving plates with home-made biscuits, Helen stood beside her, measuring milk, counting out teaspoons.

"How's — your girl?" asked Elissa. For one rocky moment she couldn't remember Charlotte's name, so she made her tone husky and intimate, to cover up. Since she'd lost herself in her private world, she too had lost touch with the world outside.

"Better. Much better." Helen was happy, for once not depending on liquor to keep her going. "They say she's almost ready to come home. There's a very nice boy, he's having therapy too. His wife and baby were killed in a crash — well, actually he was driving. He's been crazy with guilt."

"No wonder," said Elissa. She had had one or two close calls herself from reckless young drivers.

"Yes, well — But they're clinging together. Look, I don't care who it is, as long as he gives her some hope. She can turn up with Frankenstein's monster and I'll welcome him in, as long as he makes her happy."

"And whole," said Elissa.

Helen's set mouth relaxed. "And whole," she echoed. "That's exactly right. Where's the loaf sugar?"

Elissa was quite unnerved. She had made her way through blackberry and lantana and through the ubiquitous burrawong that caught at her corduroy pants and made spiteful cuts across her hands. If there had ever been a vegetable garden, or a garden of any kind, there was no sign of it now. Huge rocks, lichened, thrust out of the skin of soil at her feet. Everywhere she looked there were flannel flowers, their pale grey petals the only soft shape in a harsh terrain. Roots of long-dead trees almost tripped her. At every step she was confronted by banksias, in couples, in groups, in stands. Odd that they gave the name Banksia Ridge to a place where, by comparison, no banksias grow. Or at least, survive.

She kept on, because she had to. In a place that had once been a clearing, where the trees were younger and more sparse, she saw the first sign of habitation. She pushed her way towards a rusted water tank, lying on its side, ants pouring out of its innards. She passed a galvanised iron lavatory, barely upright, and what had perhaps been a fowl-run. She presented herself at the foot of the abode: Macinerney's shack, as Joe called it. The white ants had been at the verandah-posts; the wooden steps sagged, some of them missing. The handrail, as she touched it, gave way. She mounted gingerly to the verandah, stepping over the empty spaces where the boards had fallen through. She stood by the door. It swung on one hinge, creaking in the north-easter, that funnelled through the trees from Hammerhead. The room she looked into was half full of old newspapers, some piled up, some scattered. Above an unused fireplace filled with debris, was a blackened picture, Bubbles, she thought. She knocked, quite loudly, then averted her gaze to the end of the verandah, where a tree-tomato grew, spindly, almost strangled by a choko vine.

Slow heavy steps from the room at the back; not a shuffle, it was somebody wearing boots. Elissa, glancing down, saw boots, split open, fastened with string. She lifted her eyes to an ancient face, pitted with blackheads, a nose corroded, a mouth sucked-in, turned-down, the lower lip festered with dark red sores. My God, she thought, he's got syphilis. Or cancer of the lip. She

70

took a step back.

The old man was wearing a felt hat, greasy and moth-eaten. Why a hat? He was short and shambling, with a pot belly. His serge trousers smelled of stale urine. Bright's disease, Joe had said. He looked a sick man, just one step from a corpse.

"What d'you want, miss?" he asked, his voice eroded by age and sickness. Then he spat over her shoulder, a disgusting yellow blob that just missed her. She was rigid with distaste. How could she want anything in this man's keeping? Even his land. It would have to be fumigated before she could put her fingers in the soil.

She hesitated. Hurry up, she told herself, plunge. She plunged. "I came to ask you do you want to sell your land? Mr. Macinerney," she added, digging her finger-nails into her palms, staring into that awful face that sported, she saw now, a fortnight's growth of whiskers. He's probably got a cut-throat razor in there, she surmised, suddenly afraid, suddenly conscious that there was no human in earshot. No sound but the cries of magpie and currawong breaking the silence; and one crow carking.

He was puzzling, looking her over with a pervert's licking gaze. Only her will that said strongly, stay, kept her from flight.

"What makes you think I want to sell, heh? Where do I live then, heh?"

"My — Joe Black told me you were going into hospital. I've always liked this hill."

"It can't be chopped up, know that? The blokes from the village tried from arse'ole to breakfast time, till they found —" He shut up abruptly, probably for the same reason that she had taken off her emeralds: deception. His little jelly eyes, the colour of mud, blinked, stayed shut; opened. He started again. "Joe, 'e told you right. I got to go into 'orspital, so's they can put me on the kidney machine." He began to pick his nose. Vile, he was vile. "Yeah, well I got no choice but sell. Know what we give for this land 'ere, me and the missus? Fifty pounds. Course, that was a long time back."

"When did your wife die?" Her nostrils revolted against the stench of his clothes, which, she was certain, had never been washed since. But mixed with her nausea was elation, because she thought, she was sure that he wanted to sell the place. Now. To her. All he had left was his land and his skin; and his skin had to be worth more to him.

· "Ten years back. Eleven, more like. I been living 'ere lonesome a long spell now. Long time since I 'ad a pretty girl come to see me ... Come inside."

Did she dare? No, but she had to. He was, after all, only half-crazy, and that with loneliness. And she could always run, lucky she'd put on flat shoes. Fee fi foh fum country.

She nodded assent and came inside, to a scene of unmitigated filth; a table littered with scraps of stale damper, a floor covered with cockroaches, some dead, some alive and running.

"You bachelors," she smiled and sat down on a chair, its upholstery ripped open and rusty springs poking through. "Well then, Mr Macinerney, can we talk business? My name's Elissa Campbell. I've been — staying — in Banksia Ridge. I'd very much like to live up here. So if you're really thinking of selling now, I'd be pleased to make you an offer."

His face screwed up, he looked her over. "Funny," he said. "I was going down town soon as I got strong in the legs. Thought I'd see Stapletons, that's if they're still there. Funny you coming. I wouldn't be wanting fifty pounds, though." He grunted. "You know what the V.G. is?"

She took her gaze from the ceiling where cockroaches were crawling, huge ones with wings. As she watched, one flew out of the glassless window. "No. I don't. But I'd be glad to settle for V.G. if that suits you." Even a little more, she was going to say, but she curbed her tongue. He had begun to dribble again. She sat very still, poised between pity and horror. Pity for him, poor derelict, horror at herself, manipulator. "You'd be better off in hospital, you'd have company," she heard herself murmur. "You must have been terribly lonely since your wife died. Have you any relations?"

"Nuh. Not Effie, neither. When she died there wasn't no one to let know. So I buried 'er out in the well," he told her. "I 'adn't got no use for it since I got the water laid on. There's a power of rock, you'd be 'ard put to dig a place deep enough to bury anyone." He was nodding to himself, his lips with the terrible sores trembling. She waited for him to go on. He was lying, wasn't he? No, she was sure he was telling the truth. Who'd know or care if the woman lived or died? No one. She felt desolate, for no reason she could name. He went on. "I won't charge you extra for the skellington."

Elissa Campbell felt her head swim. Calm, she told herself, be calm, you clot. "Way I look at it," he said, sitting down, legs askew, his fly buttons off and grey bristle spilling out, "I got no choice. If I sell to you, 'ere and now, there's no fees to shell out. Question is, you got any money?"

She took out her cheque book. "I've been looking for a place to build," she said. "The — old one didn't suit my life." Lies, all lies, but let him know who she was and he'd double it, treble it, put it forever beyond her reach. "I'll make you out a cheque for the V.G. amount, here and now, if you like." She was trembling with fear and with excitement. I saw it. I wanted it. I got it. That was how Melba bought Coombe Cottage, she remembered, out of the blue. Memory, it plays odd tricks.

"What about your 'ubby?" He reached out his hand and made to stroke her fingers. "Eh?"

She pulled her hand away, pretending to hold up her wedding ring for his gaze. "Oh, he's in — in Abyssinia," she replied. "He's left it all to me."

"Well I tell you this much, missus, I like a girl knows 'er own mind. The missus, she was like you. Day we come 'ere first she pulls me by the coat sleeve, Pete, she says, we'll buy it. I'll never leave till they take me out in me corfin." He started to laugh, then it changed to a cough. Painfully he got himself up, and went to look behind a pile of papers, taller than the rest. He rooted around, then came back with a black tin box. He took the topmost newspaper, yellow and cracking, and handed it to her. "November the eleventh," he said. "All about the armistice. Well before your time."

"Yes." She watched as he opened the box, his hands quite surprisingly soft and smooth-skinned for such a leprechaun. "You have very nice hands," she said, to fill in the time and to mask her eagerness. He leaned towards her, then pulled back. From the tin he took out glasses, string for one earpiece. As he rifled through the papers he began to sing to himself, an old music-hall ditty that trailed off into silence. He put a piece of cardboard, very frayed, on the table. Then a sepia photograph, head and shoulders of a young girl, coarse and plump and very pretty. "The wife. She was principal boy in panto. Never seen legs like 'em." The photograph didn't show the legs; just the great eyes, the flat nose, the curly Edwardian mouth and round chin. A wreath of rosebuds around her ringlets. The skellington in the well. Elissa shivered.

He took out a paper from an era more familiar to her. It was the assessment from the Valuer-General's office, a recent assessment. "'Ere we go. Thirty four thousand two 'undred, unimproved. Thirty five with the 'ouse. The fellow never come right up, scared of snakes, I reckon. Thought the blackberries might rip 'is pants."

Elissa took it from him and ran her eyes over the print. It was so improbable, all of it; and yet so expected. The dimensions, she saw, were even greater than the others. A larger frontage to the road, too, but of course, in name only: more like a cliff. A very odd subdivision. But with the other two to make access possible, and this to add space — she took a great breath. And of course, he owned the most of the cairn. She would not let herself think about the cairn.

"I'd be prepared to pay that," she told him, business-like, a little reluctant. "And the solicitors can take over, if we clinch the deal now. That's if you want to."

74

Distrust flickered in his eyes. "I got no time for cheques," he told her. "I rather get cash."

"It would take a couple of months for the transfer," said Elissa, carefully casual. "So if I make the cheque out for the full amount — And I could pay you two thousand dollars in cash — extra — or pay it straight to the hospital, if you prefer. That would take care of your expenses until the transfer was fixed up." She saw the greed in his face and she dared to breathe. She was safe. "Well?" she asked. "Or am I to look elsewhere?"

"Seems like it was meant," he said at long last. He began to cough, keeping on till he dislodged a great gobbet of phlegm which he dispatched to the floor.

I'll put a match to the place, she swore, silently. The moment it's mine. She took out a pen from her purse. In silence she made it out, signed it and crossed it. Then she offered it to him. And he took it.

"I'll give you a receipt," he said, surprising her. "You pay all the fees. Both sides."

She nodded. He extracted a torn sheet of paper from the box. He took her pen, licking it as if it were a stub of pencil. Laboriously but correctly he wrote a receipt. "What's the date?"

"The ninth of November," she told him.

"What year?"

"Seventy eight. Nineteen seventy eight."

He added the date and handed her the paper. "Near armistice day," he said. His eyes filmed. "Never forget this day, sixty years back. Tom, 'e never got back. I always thought 'e would. We was orphans. So when I go, that's the end of it. Thought I'd finish it ere," he muttered. He got up and came closer. He reached for her. "'Ow bout a kiss? Seal the bargain, like."

A kiss, was that what he meant? And if he meant more, what then? For I'm certain he's got syphilis, she thought. It was all too easy. Now this is the crux. She took a deep breath. All-embracingly, she smiled at the poor disgusting old ruin that he'd just milked of his only reason for living. With mounting horror she saw that she was committed to whatever he asked of her. But outwit him she must; and would.

Lightly, even tenderly, she picked up the hand that groped for her breast. "Of course," she said, and she kissed it, and carried it in a swift gesture to his lips. "How lucky for both of us," she breathed, with the smile that sent suckers away happy. "I'll bring you the money. And I'll come to see you in hospital. Tell me where it is."

He put his hands into the box, held out the deeds to her. "It's a long time since I 'ad a pretty girl nice to me. — Doctor Alistair's got it all fixed up for me."

Still smiling, subtly changing the quality of her smile from radiance, to tenderness, she backed away. Someone had to miss out; and he was so patently riddled. She'd keep her word. And with luck he wouldn't last long. Two months, three months, I'll keep my fingers crossed the machine holds him together ... But I'll go to see him while ever he's alive.

"Goodbye," she called, from the bottom of the stairs. "I'll be back with the money. Shall I drive you to the hospital? Tell me when you want to go."

It's mine, she rejoiced, as she sped away past the banksias. To work out and lay out and dream about; and make unsurpassable. Mine.

8

Jess was coming home. Predictably, she had grown tired of the play: that was Jess all over. Afire with excitement about any new scheme, madly in love with it, not counting the cost; then suddenly, poof! It was dismal! Don't even mention it! So boring! Pfugh! So although the newspapers spoke of a nervous breakdown, of an emergency replacement, of queues of ticket-holders lined up to pass their tickets in (such was Jess's popularity) Elissa didn't believe one word of it. Jessica's breakdown was one more piece of playacting. The Harley Street doctor who issued the bulletin was probably her lover, paid for his cooperation in the usual coin. For every man in London, so the reports ran, was in love with Jessica Campbell. Like Gertie Lawrence in her hey-day: a queue at the stage-door, royalty's near-kin enamoured. Not beautiful, they said; merely heart-breaking. No voice to speak of; but she just has to open her mouth and speak the melody and your heart skips a beat. Etcetera.

"Who the hell needs to be beautiful? What's this beauty bit anyway?" queried Elissa, deliberately slangy. One of her roles that Jim rather fancied. "Hold it Jim, if you quote Tamburlaine I'll slit your throat."

Jim chuckled, well content. "I wasn't going to." He was proud of his daughter, soon, so it was rumoured, to make Sappho into a film; and to star in a play written especially for her talents. From there to the National: it was all signed up.

"Juliet. Rosalind. Portia." Elissa ticked them off on her fingers, "Etcetera." She was curled up watching television, Ka on her lap, eating her way through the top layer of rich chocolates that Jim had gone out of his way to bring her. For once she was enjoying being a sybarite. She held up the lid of the box, with the jaundiced face of the Comte du Plessy Pralin depicted there. "Look at the Comte," she said. "He's got a gutsache from eating too many of his own wares. But what a way to go!"

Jim chuckled again. He was on vacation now, and pleased about it. Term behind him. Christmas ahead. Simple Jim, it took nothing much to make him happy. He thought they might fly to Turkey. Or would she prefer Scandinavia? He remembered that she had never seen the Tivoli Gardens.

Tivoli, what was that to her now? She had gardens of her own making, spilling over, bursting into flower in her head, one crowding the other out. All the gardens of Europe thronging there.

"No no," she said quickly. "I want to stay home. I think you should stay here and lie in the sun and get brown. Travel, it's tiring. You've had a full year, Jim."

"Whatever you like, darling," he said. Cajolery, it gets you everywhere. "I've got to get on with my book, anyway. And if Jess decides to come, well there's no way I'd want to miss her."

His face, thoughtful and decent, with a worn boyishness that was appealing, reflected his pride in Jessica. Sheepish pride, but authentic. Jessica, with the aura of the London stage about her, held a new charisma. He is very innocent, Elissa reflected, almost green. Such a hero-worshipper. It was very endearing. A man so clever, yet so gullible. She bit into an apricot glacé. "Oh damn it. I thought it was pineapple."

He looked away from the screen. It was a Glenda Jackson comedy, which made him able to bear the commercials. Glenda, another heroine: such a wake-up, he said. Which you aren't, thought Elissa. You're a sucker, for all your brains, like all the rest of the blokes. For the last hour she had been drinking vodka and orange; smoking; eating chocolates. She was very slightly drunk. And happy, so happy. She could think of Jess without a glint of green: she too had her own arena, where she in turn would reign. And James knew nothing. All that mattered to him was that she was happy again; and well-behaved.

"You're very nice to be with these days, Elissa," he said

sociably, giving a small fart, no louder than a belch, which he thought she hadn't noticed. He spoke more loudly, by way of diversion. "What one might call an exuberant calm."

"Only the calm before the storm," said Elissa, stroking Ka. Soon he would find out she was telling the exact truth.

For now it was all arranged. Aunt Winifred had kept her word. And old Macinerney was in a convalescent home, going downhill fast, but probably good for another six months, said the big raw-boned matron, not hiding her approval of the twice-weekly visits that Elissa carried out. A bargain is a bargain. And oh, how lovely to have her cake and eat it. Her happiness spilled over into well-wishing. Time enough to tell Jim later. Her head was spinning with plans. Soon, soon, when it was all legally, irrevocably hers, she would make a start on it. Meanwhile, she drove in to the public library, steeping herself in the work of garden designers long dead, of authorities alive and kicking other authorities. She learned of the progression in garden planning; of Roman gardens and Persian; the formal gardens of France; water gardens; the natural gardens of Gertrude Jekyll and Capability Brown. Some places she read of she had visited; others were strange to her. But as she read and studied, certain things became clear: the importance of the long axis; the game of in-and-out; the secret garden; the climax. Always with her own site in mind, she pored over Jellicoe (she liked Jellicoe) and extracted what she needed for herself. And in a while she knew quickly whether a book or a particular garden had anything to teach her. And she made notes, separated them into compartments, thought about them, reshuffled them. She was certain now that she could bring it off. The site, her site was incomparable. As November had run its course, with Jim still occupied, she toiled up the hill, again and again, to get the feel of the land, to feel in her bones and her flesh the gradations, subtle or dramatic, in the contours beneath her feet. Each one of the lots — more than six acres, or, as they say, three hectares, in all — had a special characteristic. The old man's was grim and steeper; the banksias ruled, with the angophoras. Next to it, on the land that had been her aunt's, there was a thicker skin of soil; and from the breaks in the trees, where bushfires had left blackened stumps, she could catch glimpses of the bay below, widening out as she climbed higher. The rocks here were smaller and more sparse. And the land that held her mother's little shell of house was different again, with banksias replaced by casuarinas, that were bent into strange shapes by the southerlies. The house, she thought, would have to go. There was no way it could be incorporated into her plan, which, she saw now, demanded a great dwelling at the crest, with the sultana's balcony high above, knocking at the sky. What do I use for money, she asked herself, then pushed the question away. Time to think of that later. For the time being, she visited her aunt each time she came, picking her way through the briar roses and pinks and woodbine that would have no part in her larger scheme. As for Aunt Winifred, rising eighty five, she would have to come where she was bidden. And Jim — well she would deal with Jim later. It would be alright, it always was.

So she studied and hoped and dreamed, triumphant in the certainty that what she almost owned and what she would create there would be more wonderful than Bodnant, more dramatic than Isola Bella; not spoiled by a rabble of houses below, and the decimating of the woodland, as Lante had been spoiled. And the view from the roof; more sublime than the Sierra Nevada, seen from the mirador of the Generalife. For what the hill that reared like a volcano over Faggotter's Beach possessed and only yielded up at the very end, was the sea, unsuspected and illimitable; stretching suddenly from nowhere to everywhere. Nothing on earth could surpass that climax.

Each time she came it was the same: an amazement sudden enough to stop your heart. First the great boulders, with caves that must have sheltered aboriginals, the topmost rocks fallen into a grotesque huddle. Whenever she saw the rocks she stopped; and she heard the sound, a hollow roar, as of wind trapped in a tunnel. And yet, not wind. One more step, and another, and there, ages below her, light years before her, stretched the sea, crashing on sand, hollowing rocks. The sea, eater of time.

Each time she stood there, dwarfed; not owning, for who could own? — isolated by contemplation. Once a solitary eagle held the currents. If he had revealed himself as Zeus she would have found it fitting. She had to shake herself free. No question of the supernal: simply a tremendous climax to a tremendous hunk of earth. No more. She would have to bend every effort to make her garden worth this final revelation.

Heavy now with her unborn creation, that crammed head, not belly, she waited for the days to pass until it was finally hers; and time then to act. She worked through books; for recreation scrutinized catalogues. She could think of nothing else. She was certain of the main axis of the garden. Water-stairs, she would have water-stairs, splitting the garden in two, the water falling into a dark pool, far down. Perhaps she should use a landscape architect, to find short cuts and iron out problems. No. All mine.

Christmas grew closer. It was all arranged between Jeanie and James: they would go to Jeanie's for Christmas dinner, and drive in to meet Jess, flying home in time to join them. It had all been fixed up behind her back; sneaky Jeanie, crawling to her father, as she had done about her wedding, pretending it would all be a surprise for mama, who would be glad to miss out on the yakka. Jim, falling in. He was by now able to bear with Kevin, who was at least able to support his brood. Young men with ear-rings made Jim uneasy, but bludgers were worse. If Kevin wore rings in his ears, at least he wielded a hammer. Once Elissa, driving home from the hill, caught sight of him standing on a rooftop that awaited tiling, directing operations. He had his back turned.

His flowered underpants were pulled down as low as a girl's bikini, to show the cleft of his behind. Not recognizing him, she admired the male animal, his mop of hair, his suntanned skin. A D.H. Lawrence job, she thought, slowing down; I bet he's got a beard. He turned. Yes, a beard. It was Kevin O'Hara. When he saw her, he nearly missed his footing, but he did not hail her.

Jim was uneasy about the Christmas arrangements. "Make things easier for you, perhaps, Elissa?" he asked. He seemed to feel that she had been dethroned. "Of course, if you feel like having it here, say so."

"No, no. We'll do it Jeanie's way. We'll live it up with Kev and the kiddies," she said, her words mocking, by long-established habit; but without rancour. For some reason unclear to her she didn't want the brouhaha of Christmas here. Who knows, next year we might be living somewhere else, she speculated, ignoring, as she always did, the impossibility of getting Jim to leave Rosencrantz. Who knows, he might be ready to have a stab at living somewhere else for a while. Ten years, say. I might have had my fill by then. Or Jeanie might want to live here. Jim's crazy for the baby, he might want his grandson to grow up here. So she told herself, not believing a word of it. Wait and see. Something would point the way. We could afford two houses, come to that. Like the Moorish court: one for summer, one for winter. When the pink oleanders came out, they moved to the Generalife. Pink oleanders and cypresses and water: a simple plan. That long canal. Be simple, use repetition, she warned herself. Remember.

Christmas day came. Jim took the Alfa-Romeo, his menopause car, and they stopped on the way to have a drink at Meg's. It wasn't very festive. The children were away. Sandy was at her boyfriend's place. Angus hadn't left a forwarding address. Meg and Willie were going out to dinner; too dismal at home, they said. When Jim suggested that they could come to Jeanie's, they hesitated, then refused. They were intending to call in at various places: Rhonda's, Frances's, some friend of Willie's called old Crocko. They said they had every intention of getting thoroughly plastered. Meg looked both glossy and despondent. It wasn't cheerful, despite the holly wreath and aluminium Christmas tree.

"Christmas, it stinks," said Elissa, as they came out of Meg's house into the nasty, tidy little garden. Odd that someone with such charming taste in dress could have no eye for plants. A matter of not taking an interest, probably.

Meg had something to impart. "I heard, on the grape-vine, that Angus is trying to form a jazz group. Of course, we'd be the last to know." Because she was his mother she said, with a gleam of pride, "Of course, he's pretty damn marvellous with that awful guitar of his." She didn't want to talk about it. She added before Elissa could reply, another item of news. "Did I tell you that Tom broke Rhonda's jaw before he left?"

"Good on him," said Jim, in the true Christmas spirit. And they left.

Jim's car all but flew along the road to the forest where Kev and Jeanie had taken up house. Jim knew the way well. He often went out for an hour or two, to play with the baby, or pretend to commune with nature. This, however, was the first time he had taken his new car. They left the bitumen road, with its fringe of yellow flowers, coreopsis, and self-sown wattles, and bumped down the rutted track that led deep into the forest. Stones flew up to menace the impeccable red enamel. Jim clenched his teeth and swore; but there was nowhere to turn.

"Serves you right," said Elissa, in the manner of a wife. "For cooking it up between you. Scheming behind my back."

Jim grunted and concentrated on his driving. The fires that had raced through here in November had cut black swathes, leaving the dead trees still standing. Further along were grevilleas and blackfellows' pokers. A flock of parrots rose screeching from the stubble. Then the track petered out, and there before them was the O'Hara holding.

They had been travelling downwards. Now they stopped in a

valley, very green, charming. The calm and the seclusion, the olive-brown of the creek all pleased her. She stepped from the car and smoothed down the pale jersey of her dress. Since she had last been here, months back, Kevin had worked wonders. The four little rooms he had enclosed with a verandah, wide and commodious. Nice. The house lay bathed in a pool of sunshine, but everywhere else it was green, all shades of green. Eucalypts, thick with blossom, dripped bees and honey. On the thonged trunks grew clumps of the lovely greenish spider orchids. Elissa remembered hearing Jeanie rave about them, some friend of Kevin's had brought them from the north. Kevin had many friends.

"It's all pretty toothsome, Jean," said Elissa. The boy knew what he was doing. No children were to be seen. But when Jim got out of the car, the three girls came out of hiding, running out to swarm over him. He picked them up and tossed them high, while they whooped. Ugly little things, froggy-faced still. Somewhere back in Kevin's family tree there was a bullfrog, thought Elissa, standing back, waiting until the girls, set down at last, decided to run towards her. She had brought them books: a picture book for the littlest one, Miriamne; De la Mare's poetry for the next one; Eleanor Farjeon's stories for the biggest. Books? They did not bother to hide their disappointment. So Jim went back to the car and opened the boot. When he lifted out the doll's house their pale eyes all but popped out of their sockets. They went down on their knees in front of it, hardly breathing. He's got the right touch, judged Elissa, suddenly desolate. And I haven't.

No Kevin. But here was Jeanie, fat as ever, lush, if you wanted to be charitable, her feet bare, her dark hair streaming, her only discernible garment a loose caftan. She held the baby boy on her hip; then set him down. He staggered towards them, bandily, fell over, cried, got up and laughed. Jim's face was alight with pride. Walking, eh? He should have had a son, thought Elissa, desolate still. She wished that she hadn't come: something in Jean's setup diminished her. And Jean's face said that she harboured the same idea.

"Hello," she said, in her gruff way. "What did you get dressed up for? You'll get torn to ribbons where we're going. Jess can't come," she added. "So we won't be going in to meet her."

Jim was cast down. "Why? Who said so?"

"She phoned me. Yesterday. She couldn't get on to you. She's got some unfinished business in London. Whatever that means."

"A bloke," Elissa translated. "Or perhaps work."

"She said she'd have to leave it till the beginning of winter. Something about Stratford," said Jeanie.

Jim cheered up. The mere mention of Stratford on Avon was a tonic to him. "Probably a role opposite Scofield," he suggested.

"No doubt. Like Desdemona to his Othello," said Elissa, teasing him. "Or what about Cleopatra to his Antony? Think she'll have a go at the Serpent?"

Jim grunted. "Where's Kevin?" he asked.

"He's out in the bush, working. He's designing — oh, you wait till you see it — really it's heavenly. It's a Paradise garden," said Jeanie; very important, very smug.

So Kev had been reading up and passing it on to his wife. Elissa was annoyed, as she always was when outsiders came poaching on her preserves. For years she had cherished the words inscribed above the entrance to the Moguls' gardens: if there is paradise on earth, it is here, it is here, it is here. And now here was Kevin mouthing it. Not fair.

Rachel was tugging at Jeanie. "Get Ab, mum. He's pulling everything to bits." And indeed the baby boy was head and shoulders inside the doll's house, his fat bottom, in blue pilchers, poking out and wagging, as he plundered.

Jim went to the rescue. "Here, muscles." He put the baby on his shoulders. "Gee up horsey," he said, fatuously, and broke into a run.

"Dad's in his element." Jeanie smiled, lush, fertile, cow-placid.

The earth mum, as she called herself. "I guess he felt short-changed with girls."

"He never complained." Elissa's tone was austere. Little bitch. "Where did you hear about Paradise gardens, Jean?"

"Kevin knows all about them. He's been reading up on them. He'd like to go into landscape gardening. He really hates European gardens. He wants to teach Australians to use their own plants," parroted Jean. "Like Burley Griffin."

Oh how she wished she hadn't come. At home she was happy, full of her own schemes and promises. Not that she begrudged Kev his schemes, really: just that when you're on that kind of a roller-coaster you're better to ride it alone. She wished she could go home.

"We're having a picnic," said Jeanie. "Kev doesn't like hot Christmas dinners. He says it's un-Australian. He doesn't like English carols, either."

"Or English poetry, I suppose. Never mind, you can give the books away. Get them Banjo Paterson."

Jeanie took no notice, but ran on. "I've got everything ready, we're going down to the waterfall, wait till you see it. Kev's dammed the creek, now we've got our own little waterfall. He puts a bottle of wine in it to keep cool, like the old Italian cardinals did in their water-tables. He saw it in a book."

There's nothing you can keep to yourself. Still, Elissa reminded herself, I must be happy with my own plans. I don't grudge them any of it, really, thank God I don't feel eaten any more. But for all that I wish this day were over. She walked to the hammock, slung between two gum trees. Jeanie was still reading bilge: apparently Kev hadn't started to mould her tastes in that area. Open, in the hammock, lay a paperback copy of a best-seller, The Cardinal Sins.

"How can you stand this bilge, Jean?" asked Elissa. "Your father would reel." Her gaze travelled to Jim, still charging around with the baby boy in his arms, pretending to throw him away, then pulling him back. The little girls were squabbling, their behinds sticking out of the doll's house.

Jeanie stared, her face sulky. "I think it's super. Ponce de Roquefort is a great character. Everyone says so."

"Well, you'd better put it away before your father sees it. Or he might feel you've gone soft in the head."

Jeanie pouted and put it under a cushion. She was still pouting when the chugging sound in the distance came closer and turned out to be her friend Nora. She turned back to Elissa as the car came to a groaning halt.

"It's Nora," she whispered. "Don't mention Jeff, will you? It's all off. She's just getting over it."

"Again?" asked Elissa, bored. All of Jeanie's friends were militants or losers. All scruffy. All followers. All vocal.

Jim, quite gallant, the baby in the crook of one arm, had gone to open the car door. He took the girl's rucksack from her and stood chatting; university palaver, probably. She had dropped out of university, then gone back to finish her course.

"Incisive," he was saying. "A brilliant assessment. There's been so little done on Aphra Behn. An excellent thesis."

Elissa, sitting in the hammock, surveyed the scene. The passionfruit wreathing the verandah, purple globes wrinkled and ripe; the wooden enclosure outside, for the baby boy, filled with his plastic toys. And, of course, the wooden engine Jim had given him. Jim, his grandfather. And I'm his grandmother. Funny to think of that. We're one generation removed from the happening scene.

"No reason you shouldn't do your M.A.," Jim was saying to the girl as they approached.

"Only money." She had pimples. And scars of old pimples. And lank hair. And she also had a see-through white cotton blouse. Jim was getting an eyeful while he was offering his academic counsel. Elissa bit back a giggle.

"Teeth will help you," he said.

Teeth, what on earth's he talking about, wondered Elissa. It turned out to be something to do with tertiary education. The girl knew all about it.

"Maybe," she said. She looked as if she'd been crying. She left Jim and came to hug Jeanie. "You look great. Where'd you get that clobber?"

"Made it," said Jeanie, rounding her eyes and glowing.

"Oh if only I had your eyes I'd never get the old one two!" cried Nora.

James, hanging around, opened his mouth to utter a gallantry, but was forestalled. The master, Kevin O'Hara, came out of the bush with his machete and his scissor-toothed dog. Elissa had forgotten; yes, of course, that was why she refused to come here. That awful cattle dog, it hated her and she hated it. It bristled now and showed fangs. She pulled her legs up under her, with dispatch.

"Down!" Kevin commanded. The dog obeyed. "Good boy." He patted it. "He's trained to spy out enemies."

"Thank you," said Elissa. "And don't bother to apologise."

"I wasn't going to."

They crossed glances. He detests me, she thought. But she knew and he knew, that he was pulled to her, against his will. Like Angus, maybe: women of a certain age. She mocked him with her smile.

He turned his back on her, "Hi, professor. Hi, Nora. Where's Jeff?"

"We're washed up."

Kevin took the baby from Jim. "He stinks, Jeanie," he told her. "Go and clean him up, will you. Then we'll get going." He was wearing khaki shorts and shirt, hoops of sweat under the arms.

"I saw you the other day. On top of a house. In a G-string. You didn't see me," murmured Elissa.

"Oh yes I did," he said briefly. And their eyes met.

9

Autumn now, dew heavy on the morning grass, the autumn birds calling. She'd never found out their names, but each year they were there, mournful as bagpipes and as impossible to ignore. Cold airs behind the still-ripening heat of the midday sun. The first yellow leaf on the liquidambar. The mangoes, sweet and stringy, at last beginning to flush.

Tonight, then, she would tell Jim what she purposed, lay it on the line. For the biggest part of her life, a great chunk of it, she'd followed him, gone his pace, been taught by him, lived where he wanted, stayed put or travelled at his bidding. Now it was time she had a turn. He was a reasonable man, he'd be able to see it her way. Would he? Like hell he would. She wasn't asking him to sell the house, he was rich, rich enough to own two. Let it stay in the family, let Meg have it, she was always crazy for it. For a while, anyway. He can try it my way for a while. And then we'll see.

Elissa was elated at the prospect of the grapple to come. Grapples come in all forms; she had been preparing for this one for a week or more, turning her back on him, pretending sleep, getting up early in the morning, always forestalling him. Foiled, he was grumpy, not used to being rationed. He made sour little jokes about it. One night he brought her a bunch of red roses, and she almost relented. Very naive of him — or very calculating — with the garden full of roses, all colours. But when she pretended not to get the message he lost his temper and spent himself on a few verbal digs, four-letters, unusual for him.

"I feel like Walter Matthau when he offended his wife, ha ha," he said. "There goes my fuck for the week."

"How nicely he put it." Elissa lifted her eyebrows. "I bet she fell into his arms."

He loped off, grumbling, to hack into the orchids he said he was dividing. Sometimes he took it into his head to poke about in the conservatory.

After a week, she judged that the time was ripe. "Come home early, darling," she begged, as she saw him off. "We'll have a bird and a bottle."

He made to come back inside. "I don't have to leave yet," he said swiftly.

But she pulled the door to, and stood outside with him, her hair loose over her shoulders, her face upturned. "Tonight," she said firmly. And added. "Candles and violins. Very Hollywood." She bit her lip and blinked, oh she was in top form.

"Damned if I'll ever understand you, Elissa." He reached for her, but allowed himself to be warded off. "You've got something in your noddle, and I'm damned if I know what it is."

He came home after dusk. The scents of autumn hung, almost solid, in dark blue air. A full moon, yellow as an autumn pumpkin, as vulgar and commonplace as the scene she intended to play, swung fair over Rosencrantz. It bathed the rose garden in its improbable light, gilding roses long out of fashion: Ophelia and Souvenir de la Malmaison, Talisman, Frau Karl Druschki, Lorraine Lee. Names like an incantation; roses almost too perfumed, thought Elissa, sitting there, waiting. Dinner was ready. It only remained for him to come. Then she heard his car.

"Boo," she cried, coming up behind him, taking him by surprise. He jumped. Then he put his arm around her. Together they walked past the blackamoor, over the polished boards and the rugs from Ispahan. He was reluctant to take his hand away from her waist, but Sydney to Banksia, it's a long drive and a slow one in the homecoming traffic. He made for the lavatory.

Hair combed, hands washed (he was all but rubbing them, she observed) he came out into the dining-room. "I've got a feeling you're going to make a monkey out of me, Elissa," he said, taking his martini.

"Mmm." She waited until he had finished. She offered him the corkscrew he'd bought in Italy, a brute of a thing that he insisted on using. Sometimes it worked.

He took hold of the champagne bottle, determined on victory. Pop! Champagne squirted, practically to the ceiling. He stemmed the torrent. "Looks like an omen," he said. "Eh? Going to be one of my good nights. Alright, Elissa, we'll play it your way. What's for dinner?"

For dinner there was everything he liked, nothing he didn't. Nothing sophisticated. Fruit cocktail — "Your pawpaw, Jim, the one you planted," she told him, with intent to flatter. Chicken in wine. Roast potatoes with cheese inside, brown and crusty outside. Peas. Apple pie, spiced with cloves, topped with cream.

"It's a banquet," he said, tucking in.

"Think nothing of it." She sat curled up, watching him drink the fig coffee that he liked and she detested. She smoked, slit-eyed, biding her time. "Benedictine?"

"Yes," he said. "By all means."

He was more than a bit liquored up when he reached for her. She hoped that she hadn't miscalculated: that he'd still be able to perform.

"Come on darling," he said. "Let's go to bed."

"In a minute." She lit another cigarette.

"Elissa. I don't know why you're playing this cat and mouse game but whatever you want, you can have it. For God's sake —"

"Promise?" she asked, very casually. "Let me finish this fag first."

But he was all at once out of temper, drunker than she'd realized, much. He lunged towards her, pulling her dress off her shoulders. She heard it rip, her lovely, old irreplaceable Givenchy.

"Oh look out you bloody clot —"

He gave her a push. Yes, very drunk. "Who paid for it?" he demanded, "I'll tear it to ribbons if I want to."

The scene wasn't going as she'd meant, far from it. They were glaring at each other. He took off his glasses, rubbed his eyes. "For the last time," he said, dropping his voice. "Are you coming

91

to bed?"

"No."

He made a grab at her, knocking over the lamp that was their only light. "Want to play it rough? Right." He wasn't joking, he was furious.

She was frightened, but not ready to give in. "Think you're Rhett Butler, do you?" she jibed. She felt herself knocked backwards. When she tried to get up he cuffed her.

"Lie still you little fool," she mocked him, when her breath came back. For that bit of lip he smacked her face. She said no more. She knew when she was licked. It was —

It was a pretty good grapple. She put up a fight, to please him, but it was only a token. He ripped off her clothes — dress, pants, that was all she was wearing. The body that thudded against hers was a stranger's. Somewhere in the mêlée she bit his hand.

When he turned on the light he had changed back: owl-eyed, blinking, he was the fellow she knew by heart. And his hand was bleeding.

"Remember when Kass scratched you?" she asked him. "Oh, years and years ago."

But he didn't remember. "Worth a week's abstinence, Mill," he said. "But don't do it again." He took off for the bathroom, she for the bedroom.

She came back to him, tarted up in her rose-coloured negligee. Her act was ruined, she saw, ruefully. "Let's have another drink," she called to him.

His clothes had vanished. He was putting them on, somewhere or other. He came back in shirt and pants, armoured. "What do you want, Elissa? You can have it."

She had forgotten how important it was for her to have her way; in the rough and tumble on the floor she hadn't been thinking too clearly. And now, damn it, she wouldn't be able to get to him as he moved, vulnerable, into sleep. She pondered: maybe a repeat performance before he settled down to a night's snooze. Couldn't count on it, though.

"Darling Jim," she said, deciding on frankness. "I've been a good wife to you, haven't I? Done everything you wanted?"

He was suspicious. "Yes. Yes, of course."

"Well, now, I want you to do something for me. All that hooha, that was just to remind you —"

"Go on."

"I want to build a house on the hill. No, wait, don't blow up yet. You don't have to sell this house —"

"Sell this house? What madness are you up to? Why would I sell this house?"

"I want to make a garden on the hill. And it's got to have a mirador, you know, a balcony at the top. Or it'll be all wrong. A mirador," she said again, willing him to see.

"Using what for money?"

"Ah well, you're the moneybags, darling. I thought you might like to try something new, for once. Live on the heights."

"I think you need to be certified," he said, no longer her lover, not even her husband.

"I own all the land now. I bought some from old Macinerney. Oh Jim, please listen. I desperately want to make a garden there."

"That's your prerogative," he said, cold fish, cold-as-ice fish. "You've already got a garden here. And I'd never leave this house. Nor would you, when you come to your senses." He was a professor, instructing her again, assigning her a role. "It's just a whim. Forget it."

"I won't!" She faced him. "You can't make me. And if you won't be part of it, I'll find somebody who will. It wouldn't be hard." Then, because she only half meant it, and she didn't want to alienate him, she put her arms around his neck, stood on tiptoe and kissed him. "Though where would I find such a masterful brute?" she murmured, willing him to smile back. And, reluctantly at first, he smiled.

10

One of those no-season, no-event days. Grey weather, cold without being bracing. The sort of day to stay in bed, to pull the blankets up to your chin and to brood. Elissa, however, was on her feet. After she'd got Jim his breakfast and put the kitchen to rights, she set herself a few tasks that she'd been putting off since Christmas. The chandeliers, for one. Those chandeliers, part of the Campbell trove, had to be dismantled (dismembered, almost) every so often, if they were to shine with the requisite sparkle. While she had been busy with her plans, they had grown dingy. It would have been possible, of course, to entrust them to Mrs Tate, except for one thing; that they'd never be the same again. If you want something done properly, do it yourself, her mother had maintained. And carried it out. So, grumbling to herself, Elissa got out the methylated spirits and soft rags and tried to talk herself into believing that the job was necessary. Peggy and Guy coming to dinner next week. Better push on.

But as soon as she'd settled to it, the telephone began to ring. And having begun, it simply never stopped. First Rhonda, with a reminder about her birthday, coming up on Wednesday. Keep the day free, darl. I've got big news for you. There was nothing about Rhonda that would ever be news to Elissa, but she made the appropriate noises. Nothing on earth would keep her away. All that malarkey.

Frances next, with one of her new raves. She had just discovered Katoomba. Marvellous, absolutely untouched for thirty years, I promise you. So old-fashioned you'll die. How about a weekend's golf, Bob can make it next weekend. Leura, Medlow Bath, the names tripped glibly off her tongue. Elissa promised to ask Jim. It would be a toss-up. He was a duffer at golf, but enjoyed it. He liked Bob, but on the other hand, he detested Frances.

Marion Brackett from the National Trust, not, thank

goodness, too gabby, with a date for a Trust sortie into the country. Someone, very ill-tempered, who kept wanting Val, slamming the receiver down, and ringing again.

Who's this Val, Elissa wondered, as she took the telephone off the cradle. Enough was enough. How nice it must have been, how restful, in the days before telephones. But then, of course, the curate would have been dropping in, or the members of the Ladies' Guild. Or whatever.

She went back to her work; one thing, she was pretty quick when she put her mind to it. She had finished three of them when a bang came at the front door. Unmistakably a man's bang.

She was inclined to let him bang on, then she thought it was probably the plumber, summoned last week for a minor job, that would turn into a major if it weren't seen to soon. So, sighing, she went to answer it.

Angus. Well! She hadn't seen him for ages. She had forgotten how handsome he was and how tall. Not a beard, for once; but a Zapata moustache. And a crash helmet, which he held under his arm while he smiled at her. The Campbell height. The Campbell eyes. The Bellingham mouth. But the grin was all his own; and irresistible.

"Hello, Elissa." He stood there, looming and smiling down at her. He had dropped the auntie bit a long time back.

"What are you doing now?" she asked severely, because she had promised Meg not to encourage him in sloth. "I'm not going to let you in, I've got work to do."

"I've come to take you out," he told her. He was much more sure of himself these days; less of a boy, more of a man. "We're going to the show."

The show? Oh, of course, the Easter show. She hadn't been for years, she'd forgotten that it was on.

"I'm playing there. I'm filling in. For a flamenco player with a Spanish dance troupe."

"Where's your guitar?" she asked, suspecting him of being up to no good.

"I told you, I'm filling in. Helping out, like." Lack of grammar, that was still his scene, then. "Someone'll have one there for me. Come on, I've got to be there by twelve."

Elissa looked down at her denim pants. "Like this?" She had on a denim smock and her hair was pulled back in a horse's tail.

"Like that," he said firmly. "Come on, don't make a fuss. You'll look better than any chick we'll be meeting."

She ran to the bedroom to get her shoulder-bag, ran back to him. "Want some coffee?"

"No time."

It wasn't until she got outside that she realized he meant the motor-bike. Of course, why else would he be toting a crash helmet?

"I haven't ridden pillion for years."

"You never lose the knack." He had a spare helmet slung over the handlebars. He put it on for her. "You look about seventeen," he said. "Wish you weren't my auntie, doll."

Off they went. It was a queer feeling, but exhilarating, to be clasping a man round the waist, to be hurtled like a missile through the traffic. At risk. She liked the feeling very much. It was heady not to think, just to feel. And to bend all her efforts just to hang on. A long time since she'd stopped thinking and planning and manoeuvring. Just to be, it was a release.

At the showground he skidded to a stop. He pulled her by the hand and began to run with her towards the entrance. He pushed her through the turnstiles, leaning over to pay for her. Then he was running again towards his goal, leaping over blobs of manure.

"I hope you know the way," she panted. "I don't."

"She'll be right." As he ran he was tearing off his jacket. Underneath was a long-sleeved white shirt, pseudo-Spanish. With his black pants and his moustache he looked the part. Enough, anyway. He dumped her in the little amphitheatre and disappeared. It was a free show, so there was a fair roll-up.

When he ran out, two minutes later, with a posse of girls in lairy flounced dresses, he had turned into somebody else. José, the announcer called him. Dolores and her Spanish dancers. And José on guitar. His bow was a flourish.

Meg had said he was good. Oh, but he was, very. Guitar and player, they were one. He had the audience clapping in time. Donna Dolores was the real McCoy, better than you'd expect from that name. But Angus — José — when he played the bulerias, Elissa wanted to jump up and dance to his tune.

He got quite a reception. He came up to her after he had taken his bow. Backstage he disposed of the guitar and put on his jacket. The rhythms were still quickening his steps and pulsing in his face.

"You're good," she said. "So good!"

"It's nothing. You ought to hear José. The real José. That was his guitar. He's my teacher. I'll never be as good as he is. But I'll keep trying."

"I thought you were a pop guitarist," said Elissa.

He froze. "I'm a jazz guitarist. Also a classical guitarist. Also rock."

"You're an everything guitarist," said Elissa. "Don't be so modest."

Angus laughed at her then and took her elbow. As they walked he filled her in on the group he was forming. "It's called Halek. That means —"

"I know what it means," she cried. "You didn't invent the whole scene, you know."

They never stopped laughing. He bought chips, a carton each. They walked to the pavilion to see the fruit, licking their fingers, squabbling. The fruit and the vegetables, such a wealth of them, so many-coloured and so splendid, took them both by surprise.

"Oh, look at the wool!" Elissa wanted to shout with pride in her country.

"I like the fruit," said Angus.

"I like the pumpkins. Oh look, nectarine jelly," she marvelled.

97

She was fascinated by the cucumbers in bottles, the precision with which they'd been cut. "Look, Angus, they're practically jewels."

"Come on," he said, grabbing her. "There's other things to see."

She had forgotten how impatient young men are. She let herself be propelled forward to the shed where the cattle were couched, chewing, on short tethers. It smelled pretty high: all at once she felt queasy.

"I wouldn't mind having a farm," said Angus. "One of these days. When the group peters out."

"Will it peter out?"

"In the end. Unless we're lucky enough to make it in big. Old guitarists, they're not on."

"You'll be a guitarist. And a farmer. What else?" she jibed.

"Whatever comes up. In the end I might go in with dad. You know, the restaurateur bit. People like eating. Never get tired of it."

How true, she thought. Must be great to try one thing after another. Whatever they are now, the young, they're not stodgy. His lightness made her own scheme unbearably weighty. To be easy-come, easy-go, that must be nice.

Now Angus was eating fairy floss. A moment later, a hamburger. He tried to foist them on her.

"No way," she told him. The bumpy ride, and the cow-shed, they'd shaken her up.

Everyone else was eating. Families milled around, hoeing into chicken and ice-cream and fruit-salad in pineapple boats. And licorice, too, long twists of it. In the sky over their heads, cable-cars shuttled back and forth, half-filled with kids playing truant from school.

"Like it?" asked Angus, swallowing the last of his hamburger, grinning at her, a bit of lettuce on his white teeth.

"Oh yes. I feel about fourteen. But please don't make me go and buy a sample bag. Let's draw the line somewhere."

98

It was fun: they were happy. To be young, to live in the here and now, she had forgotten how sweet it is. Here and there were young couples, ill-dressed, but unflurried; on the dole perhaps, but not weighed down by possessions. Not to plan or to scheme: something to be said for it.

He made her look at the farm machinery; he'd promised a mate of his that he'd find out something about a tractor. She waited, docile.

"Like a ride on the big dipper?"

She put her hands together, in silent prayer. "You wouldn't be so cruel."

He relented. He bought her, instead, a beer, which she didn't much want. Then he made her climb with him all the way up the stairs to the top of the grandstand. Halfway up, he stopped and pointed out the cricket ground. He made her wait there, more than a bit limp by now, while he explained the difference between World Series Cricket and the other kind. She didn't even try to understand his monologue; but looked intelligent and admiring. She'd run out of puff. These days she had no puff left at all. What was she doing here, halfway up the side of a concrete cliff, with rusty stairs beneath her and a scanty bit of railing between her and disaster? She felt dizzy and she felt weak. She simply stood there, too limp to protest, while he harangued her.

"So now you know all about Lillee," he told her. "Little by little I'm educating you, Elissa."

She was glad to gain the top, to be allowed to sit down and look at the ring, far below. Some trotters were lined up for a race. The prettiest one, the one she wanted to win, was last from the word go. The announcer, raucous, never stopped shouting that Deedee Boy was still last. His driver was the only one who didn't use a whip.

"The whip's part of it," said Angus, in exasperation. "You shouldn't go in a race if you're not going to use the whip."

"I think you're horrible," said Elissa. Men and women, they

had different ways of seeing things.

Angus was pleased to see the woodchoppers come on. "We're lucky," he said. "This isn't the final, but you'll see the bloke who'll win it. He's won it more than a dozen times already."

Hero-worshipper. Like Jim. Maybe all men have a bit of that in them. Instead of watching all the boring things the woodchopper was doing, she watched Angus.

"He's fantastic," said Angus. "With a bit of luck I'll go down to Tassie next year and do a bit of woodchopping myself."

"Isn't it all done by machines? I thought everything was done by machines now."

"Not quite," he came back. "You must know that."

He was cheeky. He was charming. And he was, of course, her nephew. Bad luck.

It was the best day she'd had for ages. She hadn't looked in a mirror all day. She hadn't bothered to think. But all the same, she couldn't really stand the pace. She was relieved when he stopped the bike at Rosencrantz. She got off and gave him the helmet.

"Are you glad you didn't keep on with architecture?" she asked.

"What d'you reckon? Years before I'd be out." Then he said, "Thanks, Elissa. If you weren't my auntie I'd ask you to shack up with me."

"If you weren't my nephew I'd say yes," she lied. She smiled goodbye. It had been a wonderful day, but oh God, she felt sick. When Jim came home she was in bed, sore all over, quite done in.

11

When Elissa went to call on her aunt, she was two days dead.
Kylie, hungry and terrified, ran in and out, barking and
cowering, alternately. Elissa looked at the old woman's face, the
jaw dropped, and burst into tears. Oh how sad and how awful to
die alone. But I begged her to come and live with us, she
reminded herself. It wasn't my fault. She bent over and kissed
the old face, ready to shrink from the smell of decay, but finding
instead only a faint scent of rice powder and lavender. She went
to the kitchen and opened a can of dog food for Kylie, watching
as the dog ate ravenously. That's strange, she thought, one of my
problems solved: what to do with Aunt Win. But I would have
let her stay, wouldn't I? — not razed the house till she was done
with it. She wasn't sure: better leave that thought alone. One
thing she could do, however, was to take Kylie, by force, if
necessary.

By force it was. Kylie had to be anaesthetized before she
would quit the house; tied up in the garden at Rosencrantz for
long weeks before she settled to her new life. And in the
meantime Aunt Winifred had to be buried, decently, with all the
proper rites due to a survivor.

There was no one to see to it but Elissa. So she did. From the
first summoning of Doctor Alistair, the town's young doctor,
middle-aged doctor now, to the putting-away ceremony at the
plot beside Elissa's mother, it fell to her. All of it. The rounding
up of Aunt Winifred's old friends, what few were left (but all of
them ready for the revelry of a funeral). The coercing of her own
intimates to swell the numbers. She fixed it all.

Jim, James at such occasions, with his strong sense of family
and, of course, propriety, came to stand at her side, a tall, wide-
shouldered man, filling a lot of space. But the coffin, on the
contrary, was so little; there was almost nothing to put away in
the oaken box. The sun shone down hot, one of those fierce days

left over from summer. The old relics wilted and so did she. It's all been too much for me, she thought, it looks as if I've lost those stores of energy that never ran out. The garden she planned seemed a mountainous task, quite beyond her. She rested her eyes on her mother's grave; pearly marble, with the dark grey lettering she had chosen. Stella Cameron 1910-1960. And underneath: She dwells with Beauty. She had chosen those words from a poem her mother loved. More decorous, of course, to say nothing; but some impulse, stronger than decorum, had moved her towards sentiment.

The mourners all moved off, relieved that it was over, to go their separate ways. Meg, with the Campbell sense of tradition, and perhaps a fleeting affection for an old woman she had once known, came to pay her respects. Elissa greeted Angus, who winked first at her, then at his mother. Meg looked happier; it seemed that she had come to terms with his alternative life-style. And since Meg approved of success, and the group he had started was earning money, she had decided to be proud of him. So she winked back at her son, then pulled a face at Alexandra, sulking on the outskirts, her pretty figure swaddled in school uniform, her face scrubbed clean.

Elissa hung on for a moment, saying her goodbyes. She wanted to be the last to leave, after all she was the only one who'd miss Aunt Win. How sad life is, how replaceable we all are. Jim gave her a cursory pat on the shoulder and took off for the place where he was king. Everyone drifted away, talking about anything but the old woman left lying there. Theo remained. And Kay. She was glad of their company, their aura of deep content made her feel comforted. Kay was glowing.

"Come back to my place for a cup of tea," she suggested. "You look as if you're going to turn your toes up, Liss."

"That's how I feel."

Theo climbed in beside Kay. She had given up her car, couldn't possibly afford it now. All her money problems would be solved if she sold the house, divided the land and went to live somewhere else. But the boys said no — and anyway her livelihood was there. Such as it was.

"I've got a message to do first." Kay leaned out of the car window and called to Elissa. "Follow me, will you?"

She followed Kay's car away from the cemetery, down the bitumen road first, then into the farming country, which was, surprisingly, no distance away, a mile or two, no more. One of Kay's girls, Caro, the one married and expecting a baby, was living in a shanty there, in the manner of the gently-reared young. Elissa waited while Kay ran inside with a cardboard carton of something or other. Hens scattered, brown ones and white. A pony looked up, soft-eyed, and resumed his chewing. Then Kay was back and Elissa fell in behind her car, back the way they'd come, on to the road that skirted golf course and bay, to the old-fashioned street full of old-fashioned houses, one of them Kay's.

"Gosh we're lucky," said Kay. "Wherever I drive round Banksia, I think this is the place I want to live. It must be the most beautiful spot on earth."

The house was propped up. Kay had been a widow for three years now, and before that she'd put in a long stint looking after Philip. His long illness had left her poor; she worked now, sporadically, whenever she could find work not too arduous for her uncertain health. The front garden was as simple as the house; a lasiandra, a banksia, a scribbly gum. On the other side of the path was one gordonia, nothing else, taller than the house, already in bloom and dropping its creamy blossoms. It's not much of a garden, thought Elissa, but it's restful, very. The house they entered was restful, too, the furniture functional, the fabrics clean and cottony, washed pale.

"Beer or nothing," said Kay. "Oh, there's a mouthful of sherry. Don't fight about it, will you?"

They took the beer, drinking it in comfortable silence while Kay made a pot of tea. "Have it outside, eh?" she suggested. "Under the awning. It's nice out there."

So it was. The back garden, facing north, was filled with fruit trees. Under a giant lemon grew masses of strawberries, still fruiting. Kay got out a jar of strawberry jam and skimmed a bit of mould off the top.

"I did something wrong this time. It's not keeping too well. Take some home, I've got to get rid of it."

"Trying to poison us?" Theo took a spoonful. "Tastes beaut." She began to butter some wheatmeal bread.

They sat, the three of them, under the faded canvas awning, leaning back in their deck-chairs, happy to be sharing a pot of tea. Theo, the swimming season behind her, was quite fagged-out. Her mouth was badly blistered; she said it would take ages to heal. But she was jubilant because the boys were doing well at school. Predictably, they'd won all the swimming champion-ships. Jeremy was playing super piano, Jon going to acting classes.

"He's going to be an actor. Or a politician. Or a barrister."

"Same thing." Elissa lay back indolently, warmed by their cheerfulness and optimism. The good vibes, as Kev put it. Really, one should only go where the good vibes are, she thought.

"The boys' hen laid fifteen eggs. Fifteen. She's got a nest under the banana tree and she can't be coaxed away from them. But they're sterile," said Theo. "At least I think they're sterile."

"She may have a lover," said Elissa. "One you know nothing about. A fine, upstanding young —"

"Keep it clean," said Theo, who could be a bit of a prude, laughing in spite of herself. "Did you know Kay's got a bloke? Own up, Kay, you're among friends."

Kay ducked her head, smiling to herself. Exactly the opposite of Theo: her teeth had lasted the distance, but her skin had lost its bloom. We're all getting on, Elissa mused. I don't look it, but so am I. I shouldn't be surprised if I packed it in, soon. But first I'll have a go at finishing what I've started, even if — she thought in sudden surprise — it seems too big to tackle. I'd be a dingo if I quit now. She almost capitulated, almost turned to ask them for their advice, then thought better of it. They were both modest in their ambitions, except perhaps for their children. Anyway, it was Kay's show today. She had noticed, lately, that Kay was brimming with happiness and put it down to Caro's baby. But no, it appeared that there was more to it than that.

"Theo, you're exaggerating. It's just a friendship." Clearly, Kay wanted to be interrogated.

"Men aren't friends," said Elissa. "Not with pretty women. Go on, spit it out."

"It's nothing. Just a very nice widower who's bought a little farm at Gosford. He's mad about horses."

Horses? Rich, then? "Is he rich?" asked Elissa. "I hope so." Kay was bridling. "I think he is. But that's not the point."

"Of course it isn't," said Theo. "Elissa's money mad, that's all. Joking, Liss," she added, in haste.

"I'm not. It's just that I'd like to see Kay taken care of."

Kay took an apple from the pile of Jonathans on the table. "He gave me a case of apples," she told them. "Take some home with you. That's what I was leaving with Caro. How on earth could I eat a whole case of apples?" She was so happy, her laughter bubbling, her dimples deepening. "He's awfully nice. He's really taken pity on me. He often takes me up to the farm."

"Men are pitiless," Elissa told her. "Didn't you know that, you innocent? So he must be after you. Now Kay, make him show his cards before you go to bed with him."

"He's not like that!" cried Kay.

Elissa went to speak, but Theo got in first. "They're all like that. Am I right, Elissa?" She hopped up. "Got to go to the dentist and beg him to patch my teeth up again. I've got more fillings than teeth by now. Don't bust up the party, I'll walk."

Elissa would have liked to linger. She let her eyes run over the trees, chosen for fruit, not flowers. The same with the house, everything for use, nothing for show. So simple. She didn't want to leave. But manners are manners, so she got up, smoothing her dress.

"It's alright, Ted, I'm ready to go. I've got to get to the shops. And I've taken Aunt Winifred's dog, Kylie, did I tell you? She's fretting, poor little thing. Ka's giving her hell. Thanks for coming to give Aunt Win a send-off." It's strange to be one of the old ones, she thought. No one left who remembers me from the beginning. She shivered in the sunshine. Then she went to kiss Kay, truly wishing her well. "I'll keep my fingers crossed for you, Kay. It's time things went right for you. Really right."

"They will," said Theo. "I reckon."

They took their leave. From the car Elissa honked farewell. Kay had one hand on her right breast, a gesture that she had only lately acquired.

"Hope she's not too keen on him," Elissa said, after a moment. "Men being men."

"Mm," said Theo, looking out of the window. "Easily put off, aren't they?"

When she turned into her street, she saw the truck outside. The O'Hara truck, painted, for some reason, with loaves and fishes; probably to remind everyone that Kevin, the carpenter, had a pretty good precedent. Wonder what he wants, Elissa pondered, while she parked her car under the pergola that had space for another half dozen cars. But no sooner had the girls learned to drive than they had taken off. Why, she wondered, hadn't Kevin driven inside. In one of his black moods, she surmised: from time to time he really turned it on. Jeanie and all the Campbells, in this mood, became the caterpillars of the commonwealth. One day she'd had enough. Right, Kev, now we know you did Shakespeare for the H.S.C. you can get going. He'd almost taken a swipe at her, that time. Oh Lord, she thought, there's been too much drama for one day, I hope he's not spoiling for a fight. He could be fierce and he could be tiresome, sometimes both together. State the facts, Elissa. Don't bother turning on the charm. All that.

Today, shaken by the funeral, saddened by her aunt's lonely death, she didn't want to tussle with anyone. Least of all Jeanie's quarrelsome young husband. She went to the dooryard, to find Kylie and reassure her. In a while she'd put on flat shoes and take her for a walk, poor little thing. That's one thing she could do for Aunt Win, be good to her dog. Ka was sulking, whisking off whenever she came near him. Funny, she thought, as she rounded the corner of the house, I can really get going with my plans, the garden part of it, anyway, but I'm too damn languid. Let's face it, unless Jim chooses to indulge me, I'll have to change my ideas. Instead of a, well, near-palace with a mirador, I could have a folly, maybe — no, that's no good — a temple then. I could afford a small temple. The idea was so stupid that she began to laugh. Afford a temple.

"What are you laughing about?" It was Kevin, sitting on the ground, eating an apple. Everyone was eating apples today. In the supermarket too, where she'd gone when she dropped Theo, the smell of apples everywhere.

"It must be a good season for apples," she said, not answering his question. Kevin was the last one in the world she'd be confiding in. Frivolity infuriated him. He hated the idle rich, as he often told her. If he knew what she proposed, he'd want to dismember her with that machete of his.

"What brings you here? Son in law?" she added inconsequentially.

He didn't answer either. He had taken Kylie off the long lead that kept her from escaping, and was fondling her ears. He loved dogs; there was something very endearing about the way he played with them. Like a schoolboy. Like Theo's sons.

"You'll like having a dog," he told her. "If you hadn't taken her we would."

"Is Jeanie better?" Jeanie, laid low with some virus, had been unable to come to the funeral. Trust Jeanie to get sick at the appropriate moment.

"Nearly. She sent me to get her potter's wheel. She's going to start pottery again. She wants to teach the kids."

"Has she given up weaving?" Elissa moved away from him. Very sweaty he smelled; boozy, too. The O'Haras were all boozers, Old John O'Hara, Pat, all of them.

"No, spinning and weaving, they're still big. She just thought she'd try something else. She wants to start teaching Rachel so's she'll get really good at it."

"Oh, I thought you didn't believe in teaching children anything." Her voice, very sweet, held a tinge of acid. "I thought you just liked to see them blossom."

He was chewing the apple core. Now he chucked it down and got up in one bound. "You'd be just about the biggest bitch that ever lived," he told her.

Elissa didn't want to tangle with him. A good fight, yes, sometimes she liked a good fight, or a slanging-match; but today she didn't feel up to it, too wrung-out.

"I'll get the wheel. It's in the old playroom." She was very conscious of him, close behind her as she made for the door of the children's old room. She had her hand on the knob when he grabbed her, swung her round.

His clutch was a vice. He held her jammed against the wall. For one terrible moment she thought that he was going to kill her. Then she saw that what he intended was something quite different.

"Let me go," she ordered, trying to keep cool. For answer he pressed against her. Beard in her face, stifling her.

She managed to turn her face away. "I guess this is a joke, Kevin," she whispered, afraid, but not showing it. "Or I'd have to kick you."

"You've been asking for this a long time." He kissed her, forcing her lips apart, bruising her. She had played this scene before — oh, but this time it was for real. He was horrible, revolting. She twisted her head away.

"If you don't let me go I'll scream. Jim's out there, I heard his car," she lied, frantically thinking.

He let her go. His eyes narrowed. "Who wants an old boiler?" he said, back to his senses. "Serves you right for being such a cock-teaser. You had it coming to you."

She swung away from him. "Take the wheel. I won't mention this to Jeanie. I guess it wouldn't have happened if you'd been sober."

"You ought to think yourself lucky even getting a whistle from a bloke my age." He was going to brazen it out.

Kylie was whimpering. For two pins, Elissa thought, I'd join in. She turned sharply and went into the house; house like a fortress. She locked the doors, all the doors, in case he changed his mind. Really I don't feel like being raped today, she thought, trying to turn it into comedy. She heard, at last, the truck pull away, with the potter's wheel and the loaves and fishes, and the carpenter, who wasn't living up to the example he'd been set. Not by a long shot.

12

All autumn Elissa had languished, not ill, but far from well. Her abundant energies had forsaken her. She had no heart for schemes. She had mislaid the armoury of charms that usually bent Jim to her will. She felt wan. Sometimes she forced herself out to a matinée with her friends; or to one of their luncheons. She took Kylie for walks, glad that she was so easily able to make someone happy, even if it was only a dog. Ka stopped being affronted. He showed Kylie that he was master; and she bent the head. Poor little thing, thought Elissa, fondling the dog's ears, cradling Ka in her lap. She felt deeply vulnerable, full of pity for all things born, at the mercy of any wind that moved her this way or that.

Her body, that she had controlled so perfectly, that had served her so well so many years, was beginning to let her down. She had always maintained that's one's body was a machine: look after it, nourish it, and it would last forever. But now it turned out not to be so.

For what she hadn't counted on was the menopause. Whatever the doctors say, she reflected, it splits a woman's life down the middle. She remembered now those first signs she'd ignored, the clammy hands, the ready tears. It happens all ways: creeps up on you, or comes like a thunderclap in the night. One month she was functioning, as smoothly as a girl. And the next not. Worst of all was the malaise that came with it, the lassitude, the tears she had to bite back. She said not a word to Jim, nor to her friends. Ridiculous, she knew; treating it as if it were leprosy, and if she spoke of it she'd be banished to a lazaret. They give you oestrogen, she recalled, if it gets too bad; that plumps out your skin and gets your innards lubricated, gives you the illusion that you're still on the right side of the chasm. If I were a different sort of woman, maybe I'd feel less bereft. But all my life long I've traded on my well, my sex, and now I feel so sexless.

She kept Jim at bay; not for coquetry, not by design; it was just that she felt that she'd scream if he touched her. And at first he sulked; then he held himself aloof. She began to wish she had a bedroom of her own; even toyed with the idea. But no, that would be the beginning of the end. And she'd get over this feeling in a while, she'd have to.

I'll go and have my cancer test, she decided. It's well past time. And I'll ask Doctor Alistair what to do. I can talk to him. The doctor who had looked after her all these years, and Jim (not that Jim needed much patching up) and the children, all of us. He'll help me. I might just need a tonic, iron or kelp or something like that. She telephoned, commandeering the last appointment of his afternoon surgery hours, when she would be able to claim his attention for as long as she needed. She was filled with hope: someone to help her and advise her and give her back her strength.

In the comfortable, old-fashioned waiting-room she leafed through old copies of Time, averting her eyes from two wailing toddlers and a workman with a bloody rag wrapped round his hand. Doctor Alistair was running late. She waited, willing herself to sit still. And at last it was her turn.

"You're looking peaky, Elissa," he greeted her. He listened while she told him, briefly, of her symptoms. "Right. Slip off your underclothes." He indicated the couch. "Then step up lightly." He turned away, pretending to be busy with something at his desk, while she did as he bade.

"Ready," she said. She lay on the couch, arms pressed to her sides, eyes staring up at a crack in the buff plaster of the ceiling. She tried to relax as he got started on the routine that always made her feel squeamish.

It took longer than usual. He bent over her now, on another tack. He was digging his hands into her belly.

"What is it?" She sat up, suddenly afraid. "What have you found?" Cancer, it wasn't cancer?

He stood looking down at her. "Good God, Elissa," he said.

111

"You're pregnant." And he gave a roar of laughter.

She wasn't. She couldn't be. Oh yes — but she could. If the cap fits, wear it, she thought — oh that rotten Jim.

"I don't believe it!" she cried out, lying back. But the feeling that came flooding over her, it was relief as much as it was an amazement; and it wasn't so far from joy.

"Three months along," he stated. "More, probably. No doubt about it. We'll have to test for mongolism, of course. But you're a healthy girl. How old are you, Elissa?"

"Forty three," she said, not meeting his eyes, feeling like an old fool. "It was a slip-up. I was going to ask you for oestrogen or something. I felt so low."

"Well —" He was as elated as if it were all his doing. What on earth did anyone have to be elated about? She stopped feeling happy and began to see the other side.

"Do you remember when I had Jeanie? You broke the news. I'd only been married about a minute and a half."

Family doctor, he remembered it well. "You said you were too young to have a baby."

"And now I'm too old," she mourned. "Jim'll kill me. Don't tell him, will you? Leave it to me."

"I think you'll find he'll be pleased. Glad you're not talking any rubbish about abortions. You've got a good head on your shoulders. As well as a pretty one," he added gallantly. "We'll have to get you along for a check-up, see if everything's in order. Sooner the better." And because he was a man as well as a doctor, and he had known her for years, his eyes — unmistakably — glinted. He gave her a quite wolfish grin of amusement. "Well well," he said. Then he assumed his formal role. "You're over the first hurdle. You'll start to feel better any day now. You were lucky, you missed out on morning sickness."

112

And he was right: she did feel better, much better. Her eyes were clear again and her hair springy. Her waistline — how could she have been so blind? — had widened. Of course, that was the pattern. Breasts sore, waistline thicker. In twenty five years, though, you're entitled to forget. She wore caftans, full skirts, loose overblouses, that hid her no-waist. She felt her energies seeping back and her interest in living. And she hugged the knowledge to herself, keeping it even from Jim. Time enough later. And she was angry with him still: in the end he had imposed his will on her. I asked for a belvedere and I got a baby. Great.

The tests came back. Nothing wrong. And the baby was a boy.

13

In July, mid-winter, Jess was to come home, this time for sure.
The papers played it up. She had made a super-swift recovery
after her withdrawal from Sappho, which had, without her,
dwindled to a close. There was still talk of its being taken to
America, and being filmed. But the big news from Jess had been
the trio of one-acters tailored for her by Appleyard. Gogogo they
were called, each Go with a different meaning. She played a waif
in one, a countess in another, a trollop in the third. Jess scores
again. All very obvious, she had written, in her firm, dashing
script. Lovely dialogue. Next stop the National. Soon she'd have
to catch her breath and take a holiday.

Soon was now. With Jim, with Jeanie and Kevin (the kids left
with Kevin's mother, the good grandmother) Elissa waited at
Kingsford Smith airport for the machine that was bringing her
daughter back to her. So much had happened. A year ago she'd
had no purpose in life; now, it seemed, life still had a use for her.
She felt well, wonderfully well. Brimming over, like, for
Heaven's sake, a sacred vessel. I don't care if that's maudlin, I
don't care if I'm old, and a comic turn, that's how I feel. Soon, as
soon as I'm into the home stretch, I'll let myself believe it, once
and for all.

In her loose cloth coat, lined with pale mink, she sat and
waited. Restless, Jim paced. The plane was late. No, the plane
was flying in. They stepped outside to see. The strange bird,
growing larger, and the shattering noise, and then, at last, their
daughter, their famous daughter, looking just as she had looked
in the days before she was famous. No, just a bit different: the
red curls curlier, the cheekbones bonier, the step more arrogant.
And the smile, yes, that was different; wide and trusting. She
must have slaved over that smile, thought Elissa, with
amusement. Maybe, in the end, it was the smile that singled her
out. Far from naked, togged up in suede jacket and pants the

colour of honey, Jess today was playing the lady. She waved to the photographers, spoke into the microphone with the brio she'd always possessed, and, Elissa guessed (although she couldn't hear) probably a new catch in that lovely voice. Around them, people murmured that it was Jess Campbell. Jim all but burst with pride.

"She's a stripper," someone said, some hard-faced matron.

"You're mistaken, madam," he corrected her, glaring. "Miss Campbell is a brilliant actress."

Stuffy Jim. Elissa smothered a giggle. The woman quailed and moved away.

It was ages before they let Jess go. She was led to a room somewhere, to a press conference or whatever it was called.

"Why are they keeping her in there?" asked Jim, more and more uneasy as the minutes dragged on. He hated airports. He was anxious to clasp his daughter.

"They're getting her views on nudity," said Kevin, ready for mischief. He looked less feral today, hair combed, clean corduroy pants and windcheater. But whatever his garb, he was always a stirrer. "And if she thinks porn's here to stay. Rape," said Kevin. "They'll be asking her what she thinks about rape. For it or agin it." He managed to catch Elissa's eye and against her will she burst out laughing.

Jeanie was annoyed about all the fuss centred on her sister. "I wouldn't be in her shoes for anything," she declared. "All those awful embarrassing questions."

"She'll be in her element!" cried Elissa. "Just as long as the spotlight's playing on her." Despite the tartness of her words, she felt no rancour: she was glad for Jessica, to be where she wanted. Most of all she was glad to be here, stripped of spite. It must be wonderful to be the mother of a son, she thought: to feel as Jeanie feels, as Theo, as Bertha. She looked across to Jim, who looked away, hiding something. Well, so was she. Two of a kind. In the end we were well matched. The longer, though, she kept quiet, the harder it was to say anything — although, she excused herself, I've only known for three weeks, that's not very long. He's been out so much. And Jess coming. Soon, I'll tell him soon, I'll find the right moment and say it all. Or then I might just blurt it out, impromptu. I'll see. She smiled to herself, thinking of her son, and of her garden. For now Jim would refuse her nothing. How could he? But when she stole a glance at him his face was granite. He was far away in his own thoughts.

"I think you're wicked to have a fur coat," Jean accused her. "Poor little things, slaughtered."

"They're gassed very quickly. Not slaughtered. They've got horrible faces, really horrible. And they're kept in luxury. Look, Jeanie, I'm all for the whales and the seals, but if I cop it as quickly as a mink does I won't complain. So shut up, will you, and leave me warm and wicked," she said amiably.

They waited until their haunches complained. Sometimes they stood and stretched, then sat again. All of a sudden Jess was there, bursting through the door, hurling herself at them, hugging, rubbing her face against any face available, kissing anyone she could reach.

"Where are the brats, Jeanie? Oh, why didn't you bring them, you beast? Kevin — God, aren't you sexy!" She was high and hilarious, happy beyond measure to be home. She tried to lift Jim off his feet but couldn't manage it. "Three goddamned years! I must have been mad to stay away." She lapped them all in her happiness. Still the same mixture of gamine and patrician. She pulled a face and she was ugly; lifted her chin and she was beautiful. So alive: you could warm yourself at her fire.

"Well, ma?" She swung round and fronted Elissa. "What's the verdict, eh? Finished looking me over?"

"You'll pass," said Elissa.

Jessica grabbed Jim again and hugged him. "I thought they'd never let me go. They were asking the most idiotic things, oh, you'll see it on telly, quick we'd better get home to look at me. Oh Lord, I'm an egotist, listen to me."

Jim was besotted, he couldn't take his eyes from her.

116

"Sappho's daughter," she sang, kicking up her heels in a kind of Greek charleston. "Dah-de-dah-de-dah- Mother taught her, Philo caught her, In and out of boiling water. Dah-de-dah-de-dah. That was my big song. Lesbian lay, that was the other one, only two good songs in the whole damn thing. I was the lay. — Poor Maggie, everything she got to sing was a disaster. No melody. She hated playing second fiddle," said Jess, with satisfaction. "She was angelic about it, but let's face it, second fiddle to a nobody."

"You're nobody?" asked Jim, on cue. "Two ways of thought about that, Jessica."

The others in the waiting-room, those not blessed to be in her aura, listened, agog. So that's what they mean by star quality, thought Elissa. Boundless energy, boundless charm. Boundless work, no doubt. And chutzpa. My daughter.

I'm proud, she discovered, terribly. And Jeanie, yes, she's too fat, but so pretty, so sweet and ungrudging (at least for the moment) her face turned to Jess's, glowing with pleasure.

"Come on." Jim had had enough. He hustled his harem out, while Kevin brought up the rear. "Let's get home."

14

Elissa stood, gesturing in farewell, until the last one of the women nosed the last car out of the gateway. Then she spoke to Jess.

"This time last year I was so miserable that I wanted to die. News of Sappho had just hit the headlines. Australian actress in nude romp."

Jessica, her freckled face naked of make-up, her body inside the brown suede clobber as skinny as ever, turned with a swift, angular grace reminiscent of the young Kate Hepburn. She was not swelled out by success; on the contrary.

"I was terrified that you'd come home," Elissa told her. "I felt so nothing next to you. Those pals of mine, they drove me mad with their jibes."

"I bet," said Jess. "What a bunch of corpses! Ancient femmes fatales, pooh!" She blew out smoke. "I felt like farting in their faces."

"Just as well you didn't." Elissa felt at ease, surprisingly at ease with this daughter she'd thought of as alien. "We've been friends for nearly forty years, you know. You might have blown them right out of my life."

On slender freckled fingers, Jess ticked them off. "Rhonda and Frances, I'd arse them out, quick and lively. Helen's sweet, but she's a no-hoper. Bertha's alright, and Kay. Old Meg, well she's family, I guess we're stuck with her."

They had all come and looked Jess over. Two had launched darts and seen them glance off. Jess had managed to outsmart them by being so blazingly coarse that they both backed down. Yeah, she said, they all had stiffies, Rhonda. Yeah, Frances, you're so right, I was always scared I'd cop it in the eye. Never happened, though. Anything else you want to know? Bawdy, in that voice, sounded like poetry. Seeing them foiled, Elissa tingled with pride in her girl. One year. So much had happened.

Helen's girl married. Rhonda with a new stud. Kay courted, then dumped. And I —

"Kay's bloke ran out on her," she told Jess. "He didn't like it when he found she'd had her breast taken off. He told her — how's this? — he wouldn't have minded as much if it'd been both."

"Iva Titoff," said Jess. "Know that joke? Well look, ma, some blokes are like that. Weak as water. Frightened of anything a bit queer. Your generation, you've treated men like gods. They're not gods, they're people. She'll get over it. Better luck next time. I came a couple of gutsers in London. Thought I'd pack it in, but I got over it. Come on, I'll make you a cup of tea. Forget the dishwasher, let Mrs Thing earn her money for once. I was absolutely rabid for Basil's Blue Label, when I couldn't get hold of it. Funny, the things you long for when you're away from home. I'm going back like a country traveller, with a suitcase stocked with samples." She was expertly filling the kettle as she spoke, lighting the gas, getting out cups. Odd, thought Elissa, to be so comfortable with her. I don't feel she's my daughter, not really, but I think — I hope — she's my friend.

Jessica swung round, one of her abrupt movements, and caught Elissa's regard. "Like me now, do you?" she asked, equably. "Come to that, I like you, a hell of a lot better than when you were queen of the floozies. All the blokes at your feet. Dad besotted. All those absolutely sickening feminine wiles."

"It was the coin." Elissa was quick to excuse herself. "We weren't liberated, you know. We didn't know we were in chains. You know women and fashion. If you didn't get a man you were done for."

"Oh, you had a retinue," drawled Jess, smoking again. Very nice to be with another addict. "But then, why wouldn't you? You were so ravishing. You're past your prime now. Just very pretty. Makes it easier for me to get along with you. You've damped down. Thicker round the waist, too. Getting near the chop-chop, maybe?"

She wasn't being bitchy, Elissa saw, just talking straight. A nice clear thoughtful way of looking straight at you. Shall I tell her about the baby, she wondered. I'd like to, no, of course I can't, Jim's still in the dark. Anyway I don't dare, she might think I'm trying to steal her thunder, or something. I'll say something before she leaves. Not now.

"Glad I saw you in action, though," Jess went on. "Now I'll know how to cope with Cleopatra, when the time comes. Nothing like observing a really first-rate temptress at close quarters," she reflected, pouring in the boiling water. She gave a sniff, her nose almost in the teapot. "Oo wow, smell that smell! Lovely! Come on duckie, we'll take it outside. Sun's still out. Golly I missed real sun."

They sat at the iron lace table in the garden, sipping their tea. Jess had milk in first, then two spoons of sugar; Elissa a slice of lemon; Kylie a biscuit.

"You won't be able to leave this garden you know, ma." Jess leaned forward and picked up Ka. "Hey Ka, leave that lizard alone." The lizard, minus the end of his tail, slipped away. Ka, the tail in his mouth, swished his own tail in anger. He put up a paw, claws out. "Scratch me, you bastard, and you've had it." Jess put him down.

"Who told you?" Indolent as her cat, Elissa watched their by-play.

"What? Oh, the old man. We were having a heart-to-heart the other night. I don't think you realize how much this place means to him. All those boring old forebears of his — He'd feel a traitor if he left them."

Elissa watched the play of light and shadow over the girl's vivid face. "Did he tell you why I want to go?"

"He said you wanted to make a hillside garden. And a sultana's palace to crown it. I figured you were sick and tired of following the sacred Campbells. Right? He's really worried, though. He's got problems, poor sod." Jessica squinted at Elissa. "Might be a good idea if you stop giving him the frozen mitt, that's if you want to keep him." After a wait for her words to sink in, she asked her question. "Do you?"

The pigeons roocooed into their silence. Ka sprang after two pink galahs, in vain. But Elissa said nothing. Children, they don't really know what goes on with parents. Keep him, how could I lose him?

"God, I love this place," said Jess, lighting a cigarette, then putting it out. "I know what the old fellow means about tradition. It's in his bones. Mine too — I've got to get off the weed," she said, in the swift and husky non-sequitur that Elissa saw now was her custom when she was moved. "It's going to do terrible things to my voice. Can't afford that." She sat still, sunlight on her throat, the lovely childish skin of her neck.

"Jess, let me ask you something. That play, that Sappho thing that sent you to the top, do you regret it? Was it worth it?"

Jessica answered at once. "Oh yes. Utterly. It was a quick in."

"Did you feel you'd let yourself down?"

"Never thought of it," declared Jess, the ring of her voice robust. "Well, I couldn't could I? Or I wouldn't have been able to go through with it. Look, you don't know what it's like. Everyone's at everyone else's jugular. I'd had terrific notices for half a dozen plays. Then suddenly I was wading through treacle. Then here was this part. I mean, someone was going to grab it and prosper. So I grabbed. And as soon as I could I got out of it."

"You won't make it into a film?"

"Oh God no! It'll be a stinker. It's got no story, the songs are rotten. I was lucky to get the only two worth a bumper. It was flesh impact. And smut. Maggie nearly died when she found what she'd bought into. But I was glad of the chance, I can tell you that. I couldn't spare years. It wasn't the work, the waiting would have killed me. I'd have done anything they asked. Absolutely anything." She looked straight at Elissa. "You must know what I mean."

"Yes, I do," said Elissa, slowly. "More than you realize. When

I was gathering up the land — did your father tell you I own it all now, all the western side of the hill? — I had to deal with an old man — he's dead now, thank goodness — I'm positive he had syphilis — but I'd have done anything he asked — anything — to get hold of his land."

"And did you?" asked Jess, leaning forward to observe Ka's antics in the peppermint geranium. "You'll have a peppermint-smelling cat in a minute."

Elissa shook her head. "I got off scot free."

Jess began to whistle to herself. Then she pulled a rueful face. "I didn't — Not syphilis, though. Something different." She shook herself free from the memory. "Ever hear about the guy who had a taste for fellatio?"

"They all have, haven't they? — No, tell me."

"Well. He was a doctor. And he fell for a nurse."

"So?"

"Well, she was a grey nurse. Does that grab you? Sick, eh? — Well, ma, how set are you on your scheme? Because, let me tell you, dad's a hundred per cent against it. So if you want to totter on to the grave with him, you'd better forget it."

"I'm terribly set on it," she said to Jess, who, after all, knew nothing about a marriage that had lasted as long as her whole life, longer. She's warning me about other girls and age approaching, all that. But I have the key, locked up, as I always had. More now. Whatever I want, he'll have to say yes. She put her cup down on the table, that was a hundred years old, more. "I don't know if I can make you understand. I think I'd probably have liked it better if I'd been born in this generation. I was so cushioned. I had nothing to aim for. What you said the other day about dammed-up energies, well, I was like that. I had no reason to try at anything except being an — an adornment. Then suddenly I saw my way to create something of my own."

"That's your garden, of course." Jess took out a pack. "Bugger it, I'll succumb today. No fight in me." She lit up. "Go on."

"I've got to give it up too," Elissa remembered. "But not

122

oday. Well there was my mother's place, where Aunt Win was living. And the land she owned. And I managed to scrape up enough money to get hold of the other. I sold a lot of stock. I can make the most wonderful garden there, Jess," she cried, feeling the blood mount to her cheeks. "Have you seen the Generalife?" Jess shook her head. "Well, like that, only more so. Grander. And mounting views of the bay as you climb. All subordinate to the great sweep of sea at the end. The view from the top, it's got to be seen to be believed."

Jess heard her out. There was a tiny golden mole at the side of her mouth, the one she used as a beauty spot. She rubbed it now before she answered. "Well, what's the problem? You don't have to live there, do you?"

Elissa stared. "But I do. Oh, I was forgetting you don't know the Generalife. Well, it's got to have a mirador at the top."

Jess shook her head. "Are you making a carbon copy? Or creating something of your own? Anyway, the hill's got its own mirador, as I remember it. That cairn at the top. Jeanie and I climbed up to it once, years ago. And what about the materials to build the joint, how on earth would you get them up there? Bricks and so on."

"That's what I need your father for." Elissa heard the violence in her own voice, a violence she hadn't felt for months. She had thought it left behind her, but there it was, back. Ambition, drive, it's infectious. "He's got to help me work it out."

"Shell out." Jess was cynical. "You mean shell out."

"That too. And I've got to work out whether I'll be able to make a concealed driveway round the side of mama's land, or whether it's a matter of a funicular. Everything's been done his way forever!" she burst out. "Now I want mine."

"Ma, you're on a dead nag. Money and trouble both, no way. He'll dig his heels in." She stood up, stretching, her ginger curls on end. "You're screwy. Listen, that sort of place, that's for young people. Alright, so you feel you're young. But you're not."

Oh, but I am. Elissa was angry at being relegated to the

sidelines. Or young enough; and the proof of it's here. But she said nothing, and waited while Jess stood pondering, her head against the liquidambar trunk.

"In ten years you might hate the idea of a funicular. What'll you do then? You like your comings and goings, you know you do. I don't think you'd like it very much, really, to lock yourself up with a garden. Are you going to open it to the public — or what? You hate beer cans chucked around. Or are you going to do a Scrooge? It'll cost the earth to make it, and look, what about the upkeep? Thought of that? The old bloke'd hate it. Really hate it. Look, you're on dangerous ground."

Elissa faced her. "And when you stripped off, weren't you on dangerous ground too?"

"I worked out the cost," said Jess, in the end a creature guided as much by head as by heart. "I wasn't about to become queen of the G-strings, you know. And I thought I'd die if I didn't act. Do you feel like that?"

I did, thought Elissa, or almost. And now I don't. Oh God, am I so watery that I can't sustain a passion from one year to the next? "Jess, I wanted a purpose," she answered with more conviction than she felt. "I'm not just fooling, I really slaved over the plans. I wanted to make something beautiful. And lasting."

"Gardens don't last. Somebody dies and it all gets crapped up."

"So does acting. Bernhardt and Duse, they're dead. All your idols."

"Ah!" Jess caught her breath, her green eyes narrowed to flashes, her face and body quivering with sudden life. "Just to be in their company. To — falter after them!" she cried, unfaltering. Then she changed tack. "I'm doing Romeo when I go back, did I tell you?"

"Romeo? Not Juliet?"

"Both. On alternate nights. Thank goodness you made me learn fencing. Yeah, it's a gimmick," said Jessica. "Like Iago and

Othello." She wore her poker-face: impossible to tell if she were joking.

"And will Romeo play Juliet? Turn about?"

"No no, he's not girly enough. It's Fred Teasdale, very macho. No, he's doing Mercutio as well. Oh I don't think it's fair," lamented Jess, stubbing out her fag, "Mercutio's the real part. And the nurse."

"No doubt you'll play them both. On alternate nights."

Jess threw back her head and gave her peal of laughter, so well remembered, so much improved by constant practice. "Got me, ma. Yeah, I'm a greedyguts alright. Still, we're two of a kind. Well, what's your problem, really? If you want to create a garden from scratch, why not live here and just have it as a sideline? You've got a hell of a lot to start with. Marvellous bushland."

"That isn't how I saw it. It's in the European tradition. I saw it — I mean I see it as a series of mounting terraces, each one of course with a smaller enclave at the side. The game of in and out. Waterstairs, with the water finally falling into a huge pool. The bushland used as great wings. And of course, the climax of the sea."

"A mongrel, in short," said Jessica, not hiding her distaste.

Elissa flared. "What do you know about it? How could you possibly make a judgement? Any more than I could judge a hermaphrodite Romeo?"

"Fair enough." Jess looked at her watch. "Come on now, I've just got time to take you on a little excursion. Oh no, I've got to get in to the Opera House. Wait on. Tomorrow."

"Tomorrow you asked them for tennis. Your friends. Remember?"

"Yeah, that's right. Well, one day this week." She started to chuckle. "Did I tell you what old Bertha said when she dragged me into the kitchen? No? — She gave me a shake and hollered that's enough smut out of you, Ginger. I cowered," said Jess.

"Bertha's got her own talents," Elissa agreed.

15

Today, at last, Jess had time on her hands. "Get your coat," she ordered. "Hurry up. It's windy where we're going."

Elissa went to her bedroom and pulled a duffle coat out of the wardrobe. She pulled it on before the bevelled oval mirror. She wasn't in top looks today, far from it: simply to prepare the food for the luncheon and the tennis party, those piffling chores, it had taken too much out of her. Her well of energy, once infinite, seemed definitely exhaustible. I must have been worrying, she thought. All those queer surrealist dreams that kept me tossing, then vanished as I woke. Feeling that I've missed the bus, that I should have flown straight to Jim with the news. Why on earth didn't I? I can't remember. I was waiting, I guess, unconsciously, to see if I was going to miscarry, see what nature intended, yea or nay. But it looks like yea. So soon — As soon as he stops being so preoccupied. As soon as Jess is ready to leave and I've got the stage to myself. Because, let's face it, I want to be pampered and ahed over and told I'm a clever girl. I make myself sick.

She came out to Jess, sitting there in the Volvo, every line of her body expressing impatience to be gone. Kylie was whining softly, always anxious about being left.

"Don't worry, Kylie," Elissa told the little dog. "We'll be back. You look after things." She'd missed something pretty nice, all these years she'd never had a dog.

"Shall I drive? I know the way. Easier than directing you. There are two places I want you to see."

"Of course." Elissa settled back beside her daughter. "You drive better than I do anyway. I'm not in a hurry to get back, don't think you've got to speed. Jim's got an English Association meeting on tonight — or a poetry meeting. Something."

Jess shot her a quick glance, almost spoke, then decided against it. "Did you know Kevin's talking about going in for garden design? He's going to quit his job next year and do it full time. They'll live on chook-fruit and vegies," she added, uncharitably.

"I know." Elissa was curt. There's nothing you can keep to yourself.

"Oh come on, ma, you've got to hand it to him." Expert and reckless, she moved in and out of the traffic, joining the mainstream, catching the lights by a whisker. "He'll have a go at anything."

"Exactly." Elissa darted a glance at the pure profile, only a breath away. "He's a very gifted boy. In a shallow way. He's very corrupt," she couldn't help adding. Making a grab for your mother in law, it just wasn't on.

Jess, who was singing to herself, began to giggle. "Made a pass, did he?"

"I don't know what you —" Elissa started to say, then she stopped pretending and joined Jess. "You're a witch. What made you say that?" She felt very happy, sitting there beside her daughter, warmed by the full-bodied pleasure of journeying. An unknown destination, with someone you like by your side, there's a lot to be said for it. Life, it's odd. I loved her. I envied her. I admire her. She loved me. She hated me. She — I think she likes me now. She tells me the truth, that's something. You don't level with people unless you like them, not if you're Jess.

"I get the feeling that you can tolerate me, these days."

"As you said to me when I flew in — you'll pass. What were we saying? Oh, Kev. Yeah, well he made a lunge at me too. So I figured that any presentable dame in his vicinity'd get the old one two. Did you succumb?"

"Certainly not. I'm not a cradlesnatcher. And he's Jeanie's husband. And I don't think he's attractive."

"Don't you? Oh, I do, madly. But, as you say, he's Jeanie's husband."

They were skirting the bottom of the hill, her hill, so beautiful and hostile, the summit too high for her eyes to reach. She felt cold, for no reason. "There's a goose walking over my grave. I've got the weirdest feeling suddenly, that I'm taking part in something by Webster."

Jess spoke sombrely. "No," she said. "More like one of Shakespeare's dark comedies."

"I hope he won't hurt Jeanie." Elissa found herself afraid for Jeanie, so lazy and so innocent. "He was horrible. He called me a vile name."

"Can't imagine what it could be. Maybe you deserved it," Jess suggested.

"No I didn't. Not then, anyway. Least of all then. I really despise myself for even speaking to him again. But, well, I guess I had to."

"Don't take it to heart, ma. He's no worse than any of the blokes. He's quite a guy, really. Jeanie nabbed him too young, that's all. He never finished sowing the field." She honked at a car full of women bowlers, swerved; flashed a grin at a truck-driver, who flashed one back. "Old crocks in cars, they ought to be corralled and shot."

"Along with young lairs. Like you." When Jess didn't answer, she went on. "Does Jean know? About Kevin?"

"Jeanie, who knows what goes on in that skull of hers. She knows as much as she wants to, which is, let's face it, damn all. She's got somebody to lean on. She's proud of him. As long as nobody makes her take her finger out she's perfectly happy."

Elissa too, was content, sitting next to this coarse-tongued child of hers, who was hurtling her towards some no doubt terrible place for some purpose of her own. She watched the red-roofed houses flick by. They left the main road, turned into a cross-street, turned again, and yet again, this time into the winding road that led up to the plateau. Round the curve, then another, and up, and into a dead end. The tyres skidded on loose gravel and they stopped.

"Out!" ordered Jessica. "End of line."

So Elissa got out and stood looking down at a small creek, very hoarse, swollen after last week's rain, the rock faces dripping, making a little waterfall that lost itself in the valley far below.

"Not that way. Back here."

She did as she was bidden and walked after her daughter's trousered legs to a sign nailed to a letter-box, the slot covered with spider-web. FOR SALE said the sign. SOLE AGENTS. Elissa lingered, to read the details.

"Come on." Jess led the way. The terrain, Elissa saw, was almost as steep as her own, the climb almost as stiff. Steps had been cut into rock; or formed with slabs of wood, which looked rickety but felt firm. A third of the way up the slope was an olive-grey house, set on piers that looked like long stilts, the colour of tree trunks. The house merged into the trees surrounding it, hardly discernible until you were upon it. It was, in essence, a gigantic tree house. Jessica pressed on and still upwards. "Nearly there." She stopped at a place behind the house.

It was level here, flattened out and paved with rough stone, the same stone that was tumbled around the slope in boulders of all sizes. A clothesline stretched empty; two posts, a line and a dozen plastic pegs. A green plastic garbage-tin. A barbecue. An overgrown herb garden with a huge bush of Italian lavender. Before them the hill reared up, not a sugarloaf like her hill, but tall and wide, flat-topped as a drum. Tall spotted gums with spindly trunks reached for the sun. Casuarinas thickened into groves. Rocks, massive and eroded, here and there became caves. Behind them, full-circle to the east was the sea, very blue and tame, like a picture in a travel poster.

"Do you like this garden?" asked Jess.

"Very much." Elissa took a while to answer. Hills, she thought, other people own hills, or slices of hills. All the way up this pleateau, round every curve of the road, there would be more rocks and gums and banksias. "And the house, I like it too."

"Kevin replanned the garden. The house was owned by — oh,

I don't know, an architect or something. Then it was rented out a few times, with the garden getting progressively worse, more and more tarted up. So Kevin's pal got him to fix it up. He ripped out all the itty-bitty stuff and a lot of the shrubbery, mock orange and all that — See, that's where he burned it, over there where it's all black. Looks as if the bushfires went through, doesn't it? But it'll heal."

Elissa was puzzled and, yes, uneasy. Something about the place disturbed her.

"Kevin brought me here. Last week. His pal was posted to Europe. They've got to sell out. He thought I might buy it. No doubt he'd pocket the commission."

"And will you?"

Jess shrugged. "No money. Not enough, anyway. Wish I could though. I'll be based in England for years, but I'd give anything to own a bit of Australia. This bit."

"Ask your father. He's loaded." Elissa spoke up before she remembered that she too had to put her hand into the Campbell pocket.

"I did. And he's thinking about it. I could let it when I wasn't here. What's wrong, ma?"

"I was thinking." Elissa tried to sort out her thoughts, the words framing themselves slowly. "It's not so very different from my mother's house. But hers nestled into the rocks. And her garden was like this too. Cleared-out bushland."

"See that cave?" Jessica pointed. "Kev tried to grab me when I crawled inside looking for churingas or what have you. I had to knee him in the balls before I got away. I drove his truck back home and parked it outside. It was gone by nightfall. I guess he'd cooled off by the time he finished the hike back." She began to laugh. "I tell you what, it'll be soothing to get back to something tame, like Titus Andronicus."

She had had enough. She started down the slope. "I wanted you to see how absolutely bloody beautiful a good hunk of land is when it's cleaned up and left alone," she threw over her shoulder. They climbed down in silence.

"It's not a garden." Elissa was still trying to shuffle her thoughts into order. She opened the car door. "It's nature. Kevin had nothing to do with it. And I think he's an absolute lout. Poor Jeanie, to be tied up to such a —" She sought for a word bad enough to describe him.

"Man." Jess finished the sentence. "Just a man, ma. They're all lechers or philanderers, the young blokes. Always were, I guess, but now they've come out of hiding." She didn't seem perturbed; on the contrary rather pleased with the notion. "Serves me right for going into the cave. Very gormless of me. I thought because he was my brother in law I was safe. Kev's alright, really. He was just looking for a new bit of—"

"Stop please." Elissa cut her short. "I hate that word. It turns women into a commodity."

"So? Well, all life's a transaction, the way I see it. Actually I was going to say skirt. He'll calm down as the years pile up. He's pretty fond of Jeanie and the kids. And what she doesn't know won't hurt her. Don't get your knife into him, he's no different from all the young rams."

"They're not all like that. Angus isn't like that."

"Reckon?" Jess gave her sudden husky laugh.

They had taken a different route, round the back streets, making for Banksia. The old houses here, resisting the developers, were charming. Children pushed swings, or played chasings around the coral trees. How strange it would be to have a child run over the lawns again, she reflected, afraid all at once at what she had set in motion. Once I was too young, oh I hope I'm not too old to make a proper job of it. Calm down, she admonished herself. And of course it won't be at Rosencrantz, will it? But she couldn't picture a child in the garden she had planned on the heights. She sat quiet, thinking of the place they had just left. The singleness and the silence had worked on her senses, and the damp smell of moss and eucalyptus. The sudden orange of a fungus in all that sombre green had taken her by

131

surprise. The great sweeps of colour she had planned now seemed gross to her: her whole conception bogus. As Jess, crafty Jess, had intended. I won't be put off, she swore, what am I, water, to be channelled this way or that at someone's will? Jess, she'll go back to her own life and —

A car in front, suddenly stopping, made Jess hit the brakes hard. She let fly a string of ripe oaths. Elissa had half a mind to say that they'd better call it a day, that she'd seen more than enough already. Yet curiosity, or something else, a feeling that this was a journey she was bound to take, kept her mute.

They sped through Banksia, past the point where the bay petered out into creek. Little boats bobbed at their moorings, mirrored in clear water. Afternoon sun filtered through the trees, coldly.

"I missed the bay," said Jess. "Very much." She did not speak again until they were on the road that led through the chase. "You know where we're going, I suppose?"

"No. I don't."

The road stretched ahead between cliffs of vegetation, dun-coloured and olive, and dark subtle shades of green. Jess had her foot on the accelerator. The yellow line split the road in two. Hardly a car was abroad. "Great," she muttered. "We'll have it all to ourselves." She swung into a turn-off and came to a halt. "You know now?" she queried.

Elissa shook her head. "No. I've never been here."

"Yes you have. I remember distinctly coming here with dad when I was about twelve. No, wait on, you were in bed with flu. — Well, you're here now. Get out."

There were coca cola cans on the grass. "Shit!" stormed Jess. "That's what they are, shit, leaving their shit behind them." She picked up the cans and hurled them into the car. "I'd flog them till they bled if I had the chance. Come on, ma."

She swung on her heel, tall and skinny as a boy, unmistakably a girl. Elissa followed, past old man banksias, huge ones, along the rough track bordered by ant-beds. It took them a while to reach the place where the scrubby bush came to a stop. The sun had gone under a cloud. It was windy, with white clouds showing grey undersides: angry eyes observing them.

They stood, the two of them, in a place wide and flat, a giant clearing made of stone, grey and yellowish and dark mulberry pink. It was marked out in rough squares, almost tesselated. Jess took off her shoes and dragged her feet sensuously over rock. So quiet that they heard their own breathing. No birds. Nothing but their breathing and the wind in the low scrub.

"It's the aboriginal ground," said Jessica.

It was nothing. Is the dreamtime nothing, then? It seemed to Elissa that the centuries were receding into the silence, and the silence was muttering, and the muttering was a strange language, and there were stories in that language that she wholly comprehended. She stood there, silent, because there was nothing to say. At last Jessica moved away from the low bushes twisted into grotesque shapes, that surrounded the place. She gestured towards the reaches of the river, the Hawkesbury, that glinted far below and far away. She made a sweep with her arm that encompassed river and sky, and finally, the floor of the world. "There, see."

There was a fish. A shark. And kangaroos, three of them. A tortoise. Some were deeply indented, some were shallow. The black men who had worshipped there, grey-black men, they had drawn their pictures in stone. That's all, said Elissa to herself, there's no one here and they're drawings, that's all.

"It's incomparable," she said aloud.

And when she spoke she was able to observe it without her flesh creeping; and to recall what the book on aboriginal art said, that there are very fine rock carvings in Ku-ring-gai Chase. And something else: she knew now what Jellicoe meant when he spoke of the monoliths on the moors as one of the world's great landscapes.

"In springtime it's beautiful," Jess told her. "Once I came here in spring. The bush bursts into flower, just for a few weeks."

"For a purpose," said Elissa Campbell, puzzling, groping

towards something she needed to know. She wanted to go home. Here she was an interloper.

Jessica, however, had no scruples. She needed to speak. "Absolutely shattering," she said in a whisper. "That's how I want to act. Cut out all the stuff that doesn't matter. All those carvings, they're so simple and so — Well, they're not cheap. They're light years away from backers and advertising and all the rotten muck we've got ourselves stuck with," she said angrily, angry with herself. "I've had enough. I'm off!" she cried, gruff as a boy.

They travelled back fast, whizzed back into the twentieth, almost the twenty first century.

"Their art goes back to prehistoric times," Jess told Elissa as if she didn't know. After a while Jess asked, "Are you glad you came? For your lesson?"

Elissa nodded. Jess scores again. She wanted to topple me; and she did. Oh it's not fair, she thought, it's all mucked up now. I don't know where I am. What made her do it, Jess, what reason could she have? Maybe it was something Jim said, or she thought he said.

"I feel very insignificant," she told her daughter. "And the landscape I planned seems very garish. And what you showed me today — for some reasons of your own — it's all of a piece with what I'd better tell you now. I don't know if you'll think it's good or bad. I'm pregnant."

The car gave a great leap forward. Jess, looking straight ahead, gave her wild guffaw. Knuckles stood out white on the hands that clutched the wheel. "Oh God, what a turn-up! What a bloody mess you've landed yourself in, ma!" she cried. But she did not explain herself and Elissa did not ask. All she wanted was to be home.

And at last they were. Expert at the wheel, as with all her machinations, Jessica drew up at Rosencrantz. "Dad doesn't know, does he? Best you tell him," she said.

16

Jessica had gone. Like Halley's comet: there she was, there she wasn't. The plane that took her from them had dwindled to a speck. She left without furore. The photographers who had assailed her, the men from the media who had pushed microphones under her nose, they were all busy elsewhere.

She took it philosophically. "I'm an actress," she said. "Not a celebrity. I'll have to peel my skin off before I make headlines again." She was sad about leaving, excited about going forward to a season of challenges.

Her friends moved off. Jim, turning away with Elissa, looked disconsolate. He would miss her. And so shall I, mused Jessica's mother; ma, as Jess put it. This is what mothers mean when they say that grown-up daughters give them something irreplaceable in the way of friendship. My own mother, she said that.

"Coming home?" she asked Jim. But he shook his head. "You'll be home for dinner?"

"Yes, I think so. Yes, I will," he replied, his face quite severe. "Don't ask anyone, Elissa, will you? I want to talk to you."

"I want to talk to you too," she answered gaily, suddenly certain that all would be well and all manner of things — however Eliot said it. God's in his heaven, all that. She looked at his face, averted from her. "You're not ill, are you?" she asked in sudden fear, putting her hand on his sleeve.

"No." He took off in his car, red as a pantomime devil, expertly negotiating it towards, she supposed, the lectures he had to give, or at least supervise. Seminars, maybe, or whatever. She went to find her own car. There was Jeanie, just arrived at the airport, too late as usual, complaining of a flat tyre, extricating herself from a car full of wailing children. No, only two; both of them quite clean. Miriamne was teasing Ab, a little boy now. He was cranky, tossing his head and hitting out at the air. Being the earth mum wasn't such a sweet cop today, by the look of Jeanie's face. She thought she might go to the airport restaurant and have a meal. Would Elissa come too?

"Only if you need me. I've got something important to do."

"More important than your grandchildren." Jeanie chose to be huffy.

"Come to dinner on Saturday," said Elissa, to sweeten her up.

"Leave the children with me, if you like. Go out somewhere with Kevin."

"Might take you up on it. Thanks, mum. I'd better get going. I've got to get back to pick the kids up after school." Jean imprisoned a child in each hand and took off towards food. Her hair, brown and shiny, beautiful, swung down her back. The Cameron hair; by way of change. Her hem was coming down.

Elissa watched her go, then climbed into her car. It was time to have a showdown with Jim. He had moved into his study during the weeks that Jess was home; working late, he said: a publisher's deadline for his book on Middleton. There was a couch in his study, he'd sleep on that. She had been glad, for all kinds of reasons. Jess was a whirlwind, coming and going by day and night, with old friends and with new. They filled the house. It had been very nice to hear it ringing again with young voices; to hear the tennis balls whacked, not patted. Nice to have to avoid the arbours at night, with the couples cuddling, or perhaps coupling. A new generation.

Now Jess, who had thrown her spanner in the works, was gone. And it was time for stocktaking.

In old clothes, stout shoes, Elissa stood again at the bottom of the hill, observing the cars stream past, one unbroken line. Frail as a bubble, she felt the baby stir. She looked up into the lowering bushland and felt that it warned her off. Nonsense, it wasn't lowering, not even impenetrable. There was a path zigzagged out; one of old Joe's grandsons had been glad to bring his sickle and carve it out for her. It was still there, still passable; the march of undergrowth had halted in the winter. She started upwards, not too fast, short of breath before she had reached any height. She sat down on a rock, warmed a little by the late-winter sun, and waited for her second wind. The sun was abroad still, but the clouds were piling up.

Her scheme, the plan that had been for months her reason for being, seemed now beyond her capacities. I'm slowed up, she thought; it's being pregnant at this, after all, pretty unseemly age. What if Jim did say yes, please yourself, build whatever you like. Even if she somehow managed to forget the great landscape that Jess had shown her, or even, for that matter, the lesser one — even if she could forget (and she couldn't), the thought of the work looming before her, to tame this wilderness, seemed impossible. More than any one person could tackle: why then had she thought she could manage it? Before anything could be started, all this middle section would have to be razed; the trees pushed over; the nests broken; the blue-tongues. The water-stairs would go exactly where I'm sitting, she thought; and she closed her eyes, trying to visualize the lines of lemon gums, flanking the stairs. But they eluded her. — The bulldozers would drag everything out, or push everything down in their paths, and pile it all up into a pyre. She could hear the birds calling, magpies, currawongs, lorikeets. They'd be put to flight, all of them. And the kookaburras that lived in the dead angophora. She could see Jeanie's face of outrage, Jessica's concern and yes, disgust. And the money, the unthinkable amount it would cost. Jim was generous only in spasms. Anyway, what he proposed he truly mightn't be able to afford. Unless he sold Rosencrantz. And that he wouldn't do. And that she didn't want. Such an uncomfortable place here to bring up a child. Boys like to run and climb — and there's no place to run, and the rocks are too high to climb for a little boy.

So what am I doing here, she asked herself. The easy thing,

and the sensible, and the thing most indicated, is to sell it; oh no, I couldn't do that — Alright, then, keep it as a hobby. Bring in a few husky boys to swipe at the undergrowth, get rid of the lantana. What Jess had suggested: amuse yourself. I could give mama's house to Jess, she realized, with a leap of joy. She would like that, since she couldn't, in the end, afford the other one. Mama would like her to have it, she adored Jess. Then I'd only have two thirds of it to look after. With the lantana gone, the maidenhair fern would grow back again. Rock orchids, I could plant masses of them. I could plant all kinds of banksias, that orangey-buff one from Western Australia. And crimson mallee, I could plant that too. Tamper just enough to enhance, not make it tizzy. I could do, in fact, what everyone who owns a bit of land in this sandstone outcrop has the option of doing. Nothing unparalleled. Just the mixture as before.

So that was the answer then? To be glad of nature, strong and never-thwarted. To put aside my schemes, so garish and so puny, and to move with the great tides, this way and that.

She stood up. Rain had begun to fall, big drops and cold. They fell faster. She began to climb up the zigzag, for what she knew was to be her farewell to all that she had planned. She'd climb to the summit this last time, and look down on the creation that she would never create, and put it out of her mind forever. Was there time? Enough, she thought. Don't ask anyone, Jim had said, I want to talk to you. And she would tell him what she should have said long ago, if she hadn't been so stubborn. Pig-headed, not stubborn. But before she put it all behind her she would take one more look. It was raining hard now, her hair was wet, the shoulders of her jacket wet through. But she kept on. She was quite done in by the time she gained the top. Behind the last clump of banksias the cairn loomed, more sinister than she remembered, and more wonderful. And she had thought of setting a mirador beside it: ludicrous.

I was crazy, she thought, oh I wish I'd never thought of it. But then if I hadn't, I'd never have coerced Jim, and the baby would never have got started. And she thought of the baby, puny speck in all creation, but still our exclamation point. Our reiteration of life. Or stake in the future, as the Yanks put it. For no reason she remembered Professor Cameron, his sporran and his short legs, and she began to laugh to herself.

Thunder now, and lightning; more than time to go home. She put her hands on the bottom rock and pulled herself up, then on to the next one, and on. Almost at the crest, she turned to look at the sea, half blotted out. Her hand, seeking support, just missed a jagged piece of bottle. Beer bottle. Who had been here, how dare they. Private property, after all, she thought, autocrat. Rain came over the sea, wind-driven; and the sea swelled and growled. One more pull, the last one, and she'd be at the top.

She was there. She looked down from the topmost rock to the garden she would never make, trying to see it; but it blurred before her eyes. She would never stand in the mirador, smelling the hot scents of summer, fuddled by moonlight; or, at dawn, look down to the bay, spread-eagled below. It was a dream, nothing but dream. The jacarandas were only a haze. The magenta and crimson and orange of bougainvillea down there — and there — and there — melted into nothing; and the white yulans and the white peacocks — The rain, icy, falling faster, whipped at the back of her neck. Leave it.

She swivelled, to take the full force of the wind. She saw at her feet the basin of water, hollowed-out, overflowing. Her foot slipped; lodged in the pool. She wrenched it out, and wrenching, she lost her balance. She felt herself slip. Her hands sought for purchase and found none. She teetered. And she toppled, backwards on to rock, her arm taking the brunt of it, her forehead crunching down.

17

She wakened in a place that smelled of antiseptic. It was a while before she knew where she was. Her head hurt. Her arm was a dead weight: no wonder, it was in plaster. She lay still trying to make sense of it all. It hurt to think. And, yes, now she remembered waking on the rock with her arm spouting blood. Clutching it, trying to hold the blood inside. Ripping off her belt, winding it round, any old how. The terrible pain in her head. Half climbing, half falling down the rocks. Falling as she stumbled down the zigzag path and getting up and somehow making it to the road. Did I faint? I think I did. Who got me here, then?

With a sudden surge of terror she put her hands on her belly, then dragged at her nightgown. Round belly, pale thighs, dark triangle; all as before. Her heartbeats quietened.

"Nurse!" she called, imperious because that was her wont. No one answered. But it was a hospital, surely? The white beds, the tucked-in sheets, all of it. "Nurse!" She found a bell and she pressed it. Still nobody. Outside it was sunny. So how long had she been here? She lifted herself up and looked out of the window to the sea below, the toy sea, with its creaming strand and its children playing. It was morning, a new day. She pressed the bell again. And again.

The nurse who came, starchy-faced, although dressed in limp blue nylon, was sparing with her snippets of information. Mostly she wanted to repeat that Mrs Campbell was lucky to be alive. Concussion and arterial bleeding, not to mention a broken arm.

"We had to give you a transfusion," she said, with mournful pleasure. "If it hadn't been for a hitchhiker who saw you lying there, well, it might have been a different story."

Yes, one you'd like better, you ghoul, thought Elissa. "I was going to drive myself to hospital," she said haughtily.

"Morgue, more likely. Well, all I can say is, you're a lucky girl. Wonder you didn't lose the baby. Your husband, he's been near demented. He's waiting outside," she said. "Waiting for you to come to."

"My God, they've got me done up like a corpse," said Elissa, looking for the first time at the white stocks, the white carnations, the white camellias that filled the room. How she'd missed noticing them—

"They're from your friends." The nurse was sour. You don't deserve them, her face said: not flowers, nor friends, nor demented husband. "Your daughter phoned, she's coming to see you later on with the kiddies. And your friends, they're outside waiting, too."

Elissa started to laugh. In Banksia they knew everything. Before it happened. It hurt to laugh, though. "How did they find out?"

"Mrs Mackintosh was doing the library books when they brought you in. She's one of our best workers." Unlike you, said the cross face.

"Please nurse—"

"Sister—"

"Please, sister. Darling sister," begged Elissa Campbell, with her most winning smile. "Let my husband in. Just for a minute."

She relented. "Don't get excited now," she cautioned. She went out. Awful ankles, rubbery.

Elissa heard the murmur of voices outside. Jim, no doubt, was being put on his honour not to do something or other, upset her or get into bed with her, or whatever the dragon chose to decree. She looked across at the empty bed on the other side of the room. Good luck, maybe, that no one else was there, or maybe it was the Campbell money making sure of it. Thank God it's empty anyway, she thought, hazily, or I'd take up my bed and walk. Her mouth felt awful, as if she'd been eating blotting-paper. There was no water on the bedside table, oh I'd give anything for a drink of water, lime juice and water, if only I had

141

enough to rinse out my mouth. Where's Jim? He could get it for me.

Like one approaching a death-bed, Jim came tiptoeing in. He didn't look demented, just harassed. He hadn't shaved. Elissa was touched, punctilious Jim, unshaven. He did not kiss her, but stood, hangdog, beside the bed. It came to her that perhaps he didn't know about the baby, whether it was still there or not, or whether or not it had ever been. She wasn't thinking straight, still doped. Her words, when she spoke, took her by surprise.

"Oh Jim," she said. "I don't know if I told you I was having a baby."

"No," he answered, with the ghost of a smile. "You didn't. Slipped your mind, I suppose." He was very injured, she saw, nursing an enormous sense of injury.

What's your grievance, boy, she wanted to ask him, but didn't dare to send him off. She knew Jim from way back, once started he'd never stop until he'd read out the whole list of her misdemeanors. And she didn't feel up to being scolded. She put her hand up to her head, where it hurt. She gazed at him as best she could with the throbbing above her eyes. She plucked at the horrible plaster thing they'd clapped on her arm. I want to be told I'm marvellous, she thought, not scolded for keeping mum. It's not fair, he's got me at his mercy again because I'm helpless. Oh I don't feel up to turning on the charm, simply not up to it. Looks as if I've got to though. But he'd better say something pretty damn soon, or I'll start screaming.

"Rather nice, don't you think?" she asked, flippantly, trying to meet his eyes, shielded by glasses. Then she stopped pretending. "Pretty damn amazing, wouldn't you say?"

He took a while to answer. He walked across to the window and stood there, looking out, looking down, as if he were gazing at someone there below. He waited, rocking back and forth on his heels. He had on alligator moccasins, she saw. And at that moment a lot of things she'd noticed, then chosen to ignore, came tumbling into her head. Moccasins and striped silk shirts

142

and the solitary couch in the study. Oh you mongrel, she raged, and quick as a flash, no time to waste, she got to work on him.

"You were marvellous," she breathed. "Wouldn't you say it's marvellous?"

"After twenty five years it might be classed as a miracle," he agreed. "Why didn't you tell me, Elissa?"

"I don't know. I thought at first I might have a miscarriage. And then we seemed so far apart." And I was going to use it as a weapon, she remembered, with a shock. Hateful, oh, I'd better forget it fast, or it'll show in my face and he'll never forgive me. She turned her face to him, waiting.

His lips twitched. "You're going to have a shiner," he told her, and went on. "I was coming home last night to ask you for a divorce. I was going to tell you I had another girl."

Winded, she could not speak. Then her temper rose. "Have it!" she spat at him. "Your divorce and your girl. Both!"

He shook his head, moving from one foot to the other. He took off his glasses and put them in his pocket. "Don't," he said miserably. "I thought you might die."

Life, it gives and it takes away. Round the next corner, who knows what waits? Anything but déjà. She was elated to be alive, sore head, hangdog husband, baby she hadn't asked for, all of it. And there was no way any other woman was going to get him.

"Go to your girlfriend, then," she cried lightly. "Is she in the car, waiting? Go on. We'll manage without you. By the way, who is she? Do I know her?"

"Nora," he muttered, looking down at his moccasins, looking shamefaced. "Jeanie's friend," he added, to make certain she knew the score.

Elissa stared at him, unbelieving. Then she began to laugh. "Oh no!" she said. "Nora Barnacle."

"Oh yes!" he retorted crossly, almost smiling, then biting it back. "Her name's Barnes. Not Barnacle. She's a very nice girl. Clever. She's young. She's twenty years younger than you!" he almost shouted. "And will you stop cackling?"

"You go to her," said Elissa, stopping. "At once. Before she's a minute older."

"Oh, Elissa." He collapsed like a puppet, sitting on the bed with a thump. "You know I can't." He looked at her: he'd put the ball in her hands. "It was your fault too," he accused her, when she didn't speak. "It wasn't just bed. I didn't figure in your life any more. I thought it was time we broke it up. You haven't given me a thought for months. How did I know what was going on? What am I supposed to be, clairvoyant? What kind of woman are you, anyway, to keep something like this from me? You wouldn't blame me if I thought somebody else—"

"Go on," she said. "Why don't you?"

He didn't quite know; or dare. "Well, after they told me I was — well, I suddenly remembered—"

"So I'm forgiven, am I? You've remembered, have you?"

"Elissa," he said, looking straight at her. "You're a beautiful woman. You could have any man you wanted by crooking your finger at him. Don't blame me for a random thought."

She took a deep breath, her lips parting in triumph. "Finished your little fling, then?" she asked him. "Sure?" When he nodded she said, very throwaway, "The baby's a boy."

"Who told you?" he asked, quite stupidly.

"A magician," she answered. "No, the doctor. Age of technology, you know. If you're really finished with her, then you'd better go and tell her so. If that's what you want. Go on, you philanderer." She heard Jess's voice: all philanderers, ma. Of course, he'd told Jess and made her promise not to pass it on.

"In a minute," he muttered, craven. "I've been sleeping with her, you know."

"I bet you have. Staying awake with her, I guess you mean," she murmured, absolving him. The boy with jug ears, stork, the cowardly, articulate, loving bastard she was committed to, irrevocably.

"Be nice to have a baby round the house. Boy, eh?" he said, his grin beatific. "What about your garden now? Man proposes,

144

eh?"

"Oh it wasn't God's doing," she told him. "And listen, don't waste your time feeling sorry for her. She'll find another sucker."

He took her hand. There was something he wanted to get off his chest. Something wildly sentimental, maybe, kisses sweeter than wine, something like that. He bent and kissed her. "Great night's work I did there, Milly." And that was all. Then he said briskly, "There's a mob of women waiting to come in. Bertha's got them rounded up outside."

"Send them in. And get going," she ordered, smiling at him. He came to kiss her again, then took himself off, to palaver his way out of trouble.

Elissa heard him in the corridor, first greeting the women, then escaping from them. She heard his feet retreating, theirs advancing. And they came towards her, all of them, all those women of a—

"Hi, girls," she said. "What's new?"